Fairy Tales of Eastern Europe

Selected from the 1896 classic
"Fairy Tales of the Slav Peasants and Herdsmen"
written and illustrated by Emily J. Harding

Compiled and edited by Joanne Asala

Penfield
BOOKS

Dedication and Acknowledgements

For Stephanie Rebro, who traveled with me on the night train to Prague.

Special thanks to Dorothy Papich Crum, an extraordinary researcher and editor, whose people came to Iowa from Croatia in the nineteenth century to seek American freedom.

Acknowledgements

Editorial Associates: Dorothy Crum, Maureen Patterson, Chanda Hallen, Melinda Bradnan, Georgia Heald, Diane Heusinkveld, Joan Liffring-Zug Bourret, and John Zug
Graphic design by Robyn Loughran

Books by Mail

Prices subject to change.

$12.95 *Fairy Tales of Eastern Europe* (this book)

$ 9.95 *The Key of Gold: Twenty-Three Czech Folk Tales*

$12.95 *Czech & Slovak Touches: Recipes, History, Folk Arts*

$12.95 *Polish Touches*

$ 9.95 *Czech Wit and Wisdom*

$ 9.95 *Czech Proverbs*

$10.95 *Polish Proverbs*

$ 5.95 Shipping and handling to one address

$ 2.00 Catalog with complete list of all titles including cookbooks

Penfield Books
215 Brown Street
Iowa City, IA 52245-5801
http://www.penfieldbooks.com

Library of Congress Control Number: 2005909924
ISBN: 1-932043-26-8
©1994 Joanne Asala   ©2005 Joanne Asala

Table of Contents

Introduction

Sorcery, witchcraft, magic charms and incantations; dangerous journeys; unexplored forests, vast deserts and remote palaces; the triumph of good over evil; animals that can speak the language of men; the rise of a peasant-born son to the role of king; evil dwarfs, wicked stepmothers, beautiful princesses, cruel rulers, fairy godmothers, and fierce monsters—these are the themes and elements common to all fairy tales and folk tales throughout the world.

Although the Slavic tales in this collection share these stock elements, they do differ in the detail and manner in which they are told. The same tale can appear in a dozen different versions in literature, with different names and locations and details of events. For example, Marouckla, the Slavic equivalent of Cinderella, does not have one fairy godmother—but twelve! In this collection Rumplestiltskin may go by the unfamiliar name of Kinkach Martinko, but he still has the ability to spin gold thread out of common hemp.

There are many more familiar themes in these Slavic fairy tales; perhaps the reader will recognize the Greek Fate Sisters in the *Soudiché,* or Moses in the story "The Three Golden Hairs."

But who are the Slavic people?

In the midst of times long lost, the Slavic people shared a common language and heritage. Today these people are distinguished by the language they speak, not by national borders. There are the Southern Slavs who speak Serbo-Croatian, Slovene, Bulgarian, and Macedonian; the Western Slavs who speak Polish, Kashubian, Czech, Slovak, and Sorbian; and the Eastern Slavs who speak Russian, Ukrainian, and Belorussian. Each of these three groups has influenced the traditions of its neighbors, so no attempt has been made to distinguish a particular tale in this collection with such labels as "Czech" or "Sorbian."

Every time we sit in our neighborhood pub listening to the latest account of the actions of a colorful local character, or when we tell the same story that night at the dinner table, we are taking part in a tradition that is centuries old. The telling of tales is as natural to humans as breathing, and is an ongoing part of our culture. Folk tales and fairy tales teach us a great deal about past events, superstitions, religious beliefs, social customs and taboos, lifestyles and morals. The fairy tales of the peasantry often reveal a harsh world of hunger and unkindness, of violence and power and their ability to crush the daily lives and spirits of the common people. These forces could be overcome with the aid of supernatural beings who help the protagonist in the story, who is usually a poor, but honorable, person. The values of the kingdom—gold, palaces, power—are within reach of even the lowliest member of society. Many of these tales make use of the eccentric, the bizarre, and the unexpected. In telling these tales the individual is able to feel more secure in the stability of his own society.

Joanne Asala retells these Slavic legends in modern English, preserving the original richness, meaning, and magic of these "Wonder Tales." Emily J. Harding's illustrations, which were originally published in 1896, beautifully interpret Eastern European culture for readers of all ages.

Kinkach Martinko

Once upon a time there lived a poor woman who had only one daughter, whose name was Helen. Helen was a very lazy girl, and had to be prodded and scolded to do anything. One day, when she refused to do a single chore, her mother took her by the hair and dragged her down to the banks of a stream, where she began to strike her fingers with a flat stone, just as if she were beating the dirt out of a linen tablecloth.

Oh, how the girl cried and wailed. "Mother, please!" she begged. "Please stop!"

A prince, the Lord of the Red Castle, happened by that moment, and he shouted, "What is the meaning of this? What are you doing to that poor girl?" He was horrified to see anyone within his realm so abused.

"Why shouldn't I punish her?" asked the old woman. "This idle girl can do nothing but spin hemp into gold thread."

"Really?" asked the prince in astonishment. "Can she really spin gold thread out of hemp? If that is true, sell her to me."

"Willingly," said the crafty old widow, "how much will you give me for her?"

"Half a measure of gold."

"Make it a full measure, and she is yours," said the mother, who turned over her daughter as soon as the money was paid.

The prince placed the girl behind him on the saddle, dug his spurs into the sides of his horse, and took her home to his castle.

When they reached the Red Castle, the prince led Helen into a room filled from floor to ceiling with hemp, and having supplied her with a distaff and spinning wheel, said, "When you have spun all this hemp into gold thread I will make you my wife." Then he left her alone, locking the door behind him.

On finding herself a prisoner, the poor girl wept as if her heart would break. How could her mother do this to her? Suddenly she saw a very odd-looking little man seated on the windowsill. He wore a red cap, and his boots were made of some strange sort of material.

"Why do you weep so?" he asked kindly.

"I cannot help it," the girl sniffed. "My mother has sold me into slavery. I have been ordered to spin all of this straw into gold thread, but it is impossible! I can never do that, not if I sat here for a hundred years. Nobody can turn hemp to gold!"

"I can!" laughed the odd little man. "I will do this task for you in three days if, at the end of that time, you will guess my right name, and tell me what my boots are made of."

The girl didn't consider for a moment how she was to discover the answer to these questions, she merely said, "Okay, but please hurry." The strange little man laughed again, took her distaff, and set to work at once.

All day long as the distaff moved the pile of hemp grew smaller and smaller, while the skein of gold thread became larger and larger.

The little man spun all the time and, without stopping an instant, explained to Helen how to make thread of pure gold. As night drew near he tied up the skein, saying to the girl, "Well, do you know my name yet? Can you tell me what my boots are made of?"

Helen blushed and said she could not. The little man grinned and disappeared through the window. She then sat and looked at the sky, and thought and thought and lost herself in wondering what the little man's name could be, or what his boots were made of. Were they of leather? Plaited rushes? Straw? Cast iron? No, they looked nothing of that sort. His name—that was still more difficult to solve.

"What shall I call him?" she mused. "Does he look like a

Johan? A Will? A Henry? Josef? Pol? Oh, who knows?"

These thoughts troubled her so that she forgot to eat her dinner. Her meditations were interrupted by cries and groans from outside, and she peered out the window to see an old man with white hair sitting against the castle wall.

"Hello!" cried Helen. "What are you doing down there?"

"Miserable old man that I am," cried he, "I die of hunger and thirst, but no one pities my sufferings. No one cares!"

Helen hurried to give him her dinner, and told him to come the next day, when she could feed him again. After thinking a while longer about the answers she would need to give, she fell asleep on the hemp.

The funny little man did not fail to make his appearance the first thing next morning, and remained all day spinning the gold thread. The work progressed before their eyes, and it was only when evening came that he repeated his questions. Not receiving a satisfactory answer, he did a little dance and vanished in a fit of mocking laughter. Helen sat down by the window to think; but try as she might, no answer to these puzzling questions occurred to her.

As she sat in her musings the hungry old man again came by, and she shared her dinner with him. She was heartsick and her eyes were filled with tears, for she knew she would never be able to guess the spinner's name, nor of what stuff his boots were made.

"Why are you so sad?" asked the old man when he had eaten and drunk his fill. "Tell me the cause of your grief, my dear."

For a long time she would not tell him, thinking it would be pointless; but at last, yielding to his kind words, she gave him a full account of the story of the gold thread. "Unless I can satisfy the little man's questions, I fear something awful might happen!"

The old man listened carefully. Then, nodding his head, he said, "When I came through the forest today I passed close by a large pile of burning wood, round which were placed nine great iron pots. A little man in a red cap was running round and jumping over them, and as he did so he sang these words:

'My sweet friend fair Helen, at the Red Castle near, two days and two nights seeks my name to divine. She'll never find out, so the third night 'tis clear my sweet, fair Helen can't fail to be mine. Hurrah! For my name is KINKACH MARTINKO! Hurrah! For my boots are of doggies' skin, oh!'"

"You're kidding me!" exclaimed Helen. "He really said that?"

"Now that is exactly what you want to know, my dear, isn't it? So do not forget, and you are saved." With these words the old man vanished.

Helen was greatly astonished, but she took care to memorize all that the good fellow had told her, and then she went to sleep, for the first time feeling at ease with what tomorrow would bring.

On the third day, very early in the morning, the little man appeared and set busily to work, for he knew that all the hemp must be spun before sunset, and that then he should be able to claim Helen as his own. When evening came all the straw was gone, and the room shone with the brightness of the golden thread.

As soon as his work was done, the queer little man with the red cap drew himself up with a great deal of assurance, and with his hands in his pockets strutted up and down before Helen, "So tell me, Wench, what my name is. Tell me what my boots are made of!"

"Your name is Kinkach Martinko," said Helen quickly, "and your boots are made of dogskin."

The little man's eyes nearly popped from their sockets, and he spun round on the floor like a bobbin, tore out his hair and beat his breast with rage, roaring so that the very

walls trembled. "It is lucky that you have guessed! If you had not, I would have torn you to pieces on this very spot!" So saying, he rushed out the window like a whirlwind, cursing her all the while.

Helen was deeply grateful toward the old man who had told her the answers, and she hoped to be able to thank him in person. But although she stayed up till dawn, he never appeared again.

The Prince of the Red Castle was very pleased with Helen for having accomplished her task so punctually and perfectly, and he married her as he had promised.

Helen was truly thankful to have escaped the dangers that Kinkach Martinko had hinted at in his anger, and she was even more thankful in her happiness at becoming a princess. She had, too, such a good stock of gold thread that she never had occasion to spin anymore all her life long.

The Legend of
Crystal Mountain

Once upon a time there were two grown brothers whose father had died and left them with a small sum of money. The older brother invested his share of the gold, and he grew very rich—and very cruel; but nowhere could you find a more kind and honest man than the younger brother. He had a large family, however, and his inheritance was soon gone. He was so poor that he could scarcely afford to buy food for his hungry children!

The day came when even the bread was gone, and there was nothing left in the cottage to eat. So the man traveled to the home of his wealthy brother and asked him for a loaf of bread. What a waste of time that was! "You're nothing but a beggar," said the rich brother. "You're a disgrace to your family and to our father's memory! I want you out of sight!" he shouted, and slammed the door in the younger man's face.

The poor brother did not know what to do. Night was fast approaching and he was tired and cold. Yet he did not have the heart to return to his children empty-handed, and he trudged toward the forested mountains instead. Despite a long and weary search, he was able to gather only a few wild pears that had fallen to the ground. He quickly ate one and put the rest in his sack.

The east wind picked up strength, its icy blast piercing him through and through. He pulled his ragged cloak closer around him and shivered. "What am I to do?" he moaned. "What is to become of us? How will we survive without food?"

Just then the path opened up into a meadow, and before him stood Crystal Mountain. Local legend said that the top of the mountain was made of crystal, and a fire burned upon it continuously. "I will never make it back home tonight," the man thought to himself. "My only chance to keep from freezing to death is to find that fire."

He continued to follow the path higher and higher up the mountain, and when he reached the very top, he was startled to discover twelve robed figures sitting around a large bonfire. He hesitated a moment, but then he thought, "What have I got to lose? God is with me, and I should not fear the unknown. Courage!"

He stepped up to the fire and bowed low before the seated figures. "Good people," he said, "please take pity on me. I am very poor, and have no one to turn to. I am far from my own hearth, and all I ask is that I may warm myself at your fire."

At first no one spoke, but then one of the figures removed her hood and smiled. She had such a kind and gentle face, and she said to the shivering man, "My son, come join our circle. Sit down and make yourself comfortable."

The younger brother sat down, and soon began to feel warm and cozy. But he did not dare speak while the others remained so silent. They were a strange lot, and the man did not know what to make of them. What astonished him the most was that they changed seats continuously, one after the other, each one passing round the fire only to come back to his own place.

When it seemed to be his turn, he stood and stepped nearer the fire pit. An old man with a long white beard and bald head arose from the flames and spoke in a deep, rumbling voice, "Man, do not waste your time here. Go home, work and live an honest life. Take as many embers as you need. We have more than enough." Then he sank back into the flames and disappeared. The robed figures filled the younger brother's sack with glowing coals, and helped him get it over his shoulders.

"You should hurry home now," they each told him. "Your family awaits you."

Thanking them, the man set off. He would have thought for sure that the coals would burn right through the leather, but

they did not; nor did they feel as heavy as he thought they should.

When he got home he called to his children, "Come! Gather 'round! I have coals to light the fire with! We shall all be warm tonight!" But imagine his astonishment when he found the sack to contain gold pieces, and not embers! He had never seen so much money in all of his life! He bowed his head in prayer, and thanked those who had been so ready to help him in his need.

He was rich now, very rich, and he was able to feed and clothe his family in style. He figured he had enough money to provide for all of them until the end of their days. Being curious to know just how many gold pieces there were, but not knowing how to count, he sent one of his children to his rich brother to ask if they might perhaps borrow his quart measure.

"What can such beggars as you have to measure?" the cruel man sneered at the little boy.

"O-o-our n-neighbor owes us s-s-some w-wheat," the little boy stammered. "W-we w-want to be sure she r-r-returns us the right quantity."

The rich brother was puzzled and, suspecting a lie, he decided to let his nephew take the quart measure back with him. But first he smeared the inside with grease. The trick succeeded, for on getting the measure back he found a gold piece sticking to it. He was completely shocked and amazed. "My brother has joined a band of robbers! It's the only possible explanation!"

He hurried to the cottage of his younger brother. "If you don't tell me where you got this gold from," he said, "I'll drag you on down to the sheriff."

The younger man was troubled, and not wishing to offend his brother, he told him all about his adventure on Crystal Mountain.

The elder brother was a very rich man and he did not need any more gold for himself, yet he was jealous of his brother's good fortune, and of the ease with which he gained the neighbors' respect. At last he decided to make a visit to Crystal Mountain himself. "I just may meet with the same good luck as my brother!" he grinned.

He climbed to the top of the mountain and there found the twelve robed figures seated round the fire just as his brother had described them. He ran forward and said, "I beg of you, my fine fellows, to let me warm myself. It is bitterly cold, and I am a poor homeless wanderer."

"Ha!" One of the figures stepped forward and said in a voice as chill as the grave, "My son, you were born under a favorable sky and you grew rich—but you are a miser; you are cruel; and you have dared to lie to us. You will get exactly as you deserve."

Too terrified to move, the older brother stayed rooted to the spot, unable to speak. He watched as the twelve figures changed places one after another, each one at last returning to his own seat. Then from the midst of the flames rose the white-bearded old man. He spoke in a rumbling voice, "Woe unto the wicked! Your brother is a virtuous and honest man, therefore I blessed him. But you, you are wicked to the core, and shall not escape our vengeance."

At these words the twelve robed figures stood. The first seized the unfortunate man and struck him, and passed him on to the second; the second struck him and passed him on to the third; and so did they all in their turn until he was given up to the old man, and the Wizard of Crystal Mountain disappeared with him into the fire.

Days, weeks, months went by, but the rich man never returned, and no one could say with certainty what became of him. I think, however, between you and me, that the younger brother had his suspicions—suspicions he wisely kept to himself.

The Black Thread

There was once a married couple who loved each other very much. The husband would not have traded his wife for all the gold in the world, and she felt the same toward him. They were very happy together, and lived like two grains on one ear of corn.

One day while working in his field, the husband was overcome with a sudden urge to see his wife; so without waiting for the hour of sunset, he ran home. But she was not there! He looked high and he looked low, he searched all of the rooms and the yard and the stables, he wept and he cried out her name, yet it was all in vain. She was not at home, nor at the neighbors, nor in the village. His dear wife was simply not to be found.

The poor man was so heartbroken that he could not eat or sleep. He thought of nothing except the loss of his wife, and how he could find her again. At length he decided the only thing to do would be to leave the farm and travel the world in search of her. He began to walk straight down the road, trusting in the Lord to guide his steps.

Sad and withdrawn, he wandered for many days until he reached a cottage on the banks of a large lake. There he stopped, hoping against hope that the people who lived there would have news to tell him. He tried to step over the threshold of the cottage, but was prevented by a woman who blocked the door.

"What do you want here, you scoundrel?" she demanded. "If my husband finds you here, he'll kill you without hesitation."

"Who is this husband of yours who has no respect for travelers?"

"What!" the woman cried out in amazement. "You mean you don't know? My husband is the great Water-King!

Everything that lives beneath the waves obeys him. You must leave quickly! If he finds you here he will devour you in an instant."

"Perhaps he will take pity on me when he hears my story. Could you hide me somewhere? I am all worn out from walking, and without shelter for the night."

The Water-Queen was persuaded, and she hid him behind her cookstove. Almost immediately the Water-King entered the room. He had barely stepped foot inside when he shouted, "Wife! There is a human here, the smell of Christian blood makes my stomach rumble in hunger. Give him to me quickly, for I am starving!" The Queen dared not disobey her husband, and so she was forced to reveal the traveler's hiding place. The poor man was terribly frightened, and his every limb trembled and shook.

"I-I assure you I have done no harm," he quickly said. "I came here in search of news of my poor wife. I beg of you to help me find her, please, for I do not think I can live without her!"

"Well," replied the Water-King, "I have a soft spot when it comes to matters of true love. It is obvious that you are devoted to your wife, and I will forgive you for coming here. I would help you if I could, but I do not know where she is." He paused and a thoughtful expression crossed his face. "Yet now that I think about it, I did see two strange ducks on the water yesterday, perhaps she is one of them? I think the best bet is for you to ask my brother the Fire-King for advice. He may be able to tell you more."

Happy to have escaped with his life, the man thanked the Water-King and set off to find the Fire-King. Luckily the Fire-King did not have the same appetite for human flesh, but he could only advise the man to consult with his older brother, the Air-King. The Air-King, although he traveled all over the earth, could only say that he thought he had seen a woman at the foot of the Crystal Mountain.

The husband was delighted at the news, for Crystal

Mountain was within a day's journey of his cottage, and he went immediately to seek his wife at the foot of the mountain. He began to ascend the path that ran up alongside the river. Several ducks were swimming in a nearby pool, and one of them called out, "My good man, don't go up there! You'll surely be killed."

But the man walked fearlessly on until he came to some thatched cottages, at the largest of which he stopped. From the cottage emerged a crowd of hideous witches and warlocks; they surrounded him and called out his name in screeching, shrieking voices, "Jan, Jan, what is it you are looking for?"

"My wife," he said, trying hard to keep the tremor from his voice.

"Your wife, is it?" one of the witches howled. "Oh, she is here with us, safe and sound, safe and sound. But you cannot take her home with you unless you can first select her from among two hundred other women."

"That should be no problem," Jan said, "I'd know my own wife anywhere."

"From among two hundred women *who look exactly like her?*"

Dozens of women appeared from the surrounding cottages, each one exactly like his wife in form and figure. He looked each of them in the eye, and then smiled. "What?" he laughed. "You do not think I would recognize own wife? Why, she is right here," he said as he reached to the one whom he had married. She kissed him on the cheek and held him close, then she whispered:

"My darling, though you knew me today, I doubt whether you will tomorrow, for there will be many hundreds more of us, each alike. Now I will tell you what to do: at nightfall go to the very top of Crystal Mountain, where dwells the King of Time and his court. Ask him how you may help me. If you are good and honest, which I know you to be, he will tell you what to do. If you are untruthful, he will devour you in one great mouthful."

"I will do as you ask, my dear one," he whispered back. "I am still confused, however. Why did you leave me suddenly? Why? If you only knew how much I have suffered trying to find you! I have searched all over the countryside for you!"

"I know," she sighed. "I did not leave you willingly. A countryman asked me to come and look at the mountain torrent; he said there was something strange about it. When I got there, he sprinkled water over himself, and at once wings grew out of his shoulders, and he soon changed into a drake. I became a duck at the same time. I knew the only way I would regain my human form was to follow him. When we swam all the way to this village, I became human again. Now I only need you to recognize me tomorrow to go free."

"Why are they testing us?" asked the man. His wife shrugged.

They parted company, she joining the other women, and he continuing on up to the Crystal Mountain. At the top he saw twelve strange beings sitting round a large fire. They were the attendants to the great wizard, the King of Time. The man saluted them with respect and bowed low.

"What do you want?" he was asked.

"I have lost my dear, darling wife," he said. "Can you tell me how to recognize her among two thousand other women, each one like the last?"

"No," they told him, "but perhaps our King can."

There arose from the midst of the flames an old, old man with a bald head and a long white beard. "Though each of these women will look alike in form and figure, only your wife will have a black thread in the shoe of her right foot." So saying, the man vanished back into the flames, and the traveler, thanking the twelve robed figures, descended the mountain.

Sure it is that without the black thread the man would not have been able to recognize his wife. And though the witches tried to hide her and make her one of their own, the terrible spell was shattered. The wife and her husband returned to their home, rejoicing in each other, and there they lived happily till the end of their days.

Marouckla and the Twelve Months

There was once a widow who had both a daughter and a stepdaughter. Helen, the youngest, was her child by her dead husband, and Marouckla was his daughter by his first wife. The widow loved Helen, but could not stand the orphaned Marouckla. She was far prettier than her half-sister, and she was a sweet girl who never gave a thought to her good looks. She could not understand why her stepmother should frown at the mere sight of her.

The dirtiest chores and the hardest work always fell to Marouckla. She cleaned all of the rooms, did the cooking, washing and sewing, spun, wove, brought in the hay, and milked the cow—all without the help of Helen. And how did the younger sister spend her time? She did nothing but try on pretty clothes and gaze at her reflection in the mirror. Marouckla had every reason to complain, but she never did. She suffered her stepmother's scoldings and bad temper with a patience that only served to annoy the widow more. The old woman became even more tyrannical and moody, and to make matters worse, Marouckla only grew more lovely every day while Helen's ugliness increased.

The stepmother at last came to the conclusion that the only course of action was to get rid of Marouckla; as long as she was in the house, Helen would have no suitors. The widow used every means available to make the girl's life miserable—hunger, abuse, neglect, and beatings. The most horrible of men could not have been more mercilessly cruel than the wicked old widow. But despite all her hardships, Marouckla grew ever sweeter and more charming.

One day in the middle of winter, Helen decided that she needed some violets. "Marouckla," she said, "I want you to go into the forest and gather some violets. I wish to dress my hair with them, for they will perfectly match the shade of my new dancing gown."

"But my sister," Marouckla laughed, "who ever heard of violets blooming in winter?"

"Do you dare to disobey me? You spiteful wench! You miserable wretched creature!"

"But . . ."

"Marouckla," scolded the widow, "did you not hear your sister? Not another word now, off with you! If you do not bring back some violets from the mountain forest, you can forget about coming home tonight." With vigorous blows the women chased Marouckla out the door, not even allowing her to grab her cloak. "There," said the widow, "and if you come back with an empty basket, you may be sure that I shall kill you myself."

The weeping girl made her way to the mountain. The snow lay deep, and there was no trace of another human being. Who would be out in such weather? Long did the poor girl wander here and there, knowing she would never be able to find any violets. Very soon she lost her way. She was hungry, tired, and she shivered with the cold. Was she to die here all alone?

Suddenly she saw a light in the distance. Thinking that it must be a mountain cottage, she climbed toward it. She climbed and she climbed until she reached the very top of the peak. On the highest bluff burned a large fire, and surrounding it were twelve blocks of stone, each with a robed figure seated upon it. Of these strange beings three had white hair, three were middle-aged, three were youthful and handsome, and the rest were even younger still. "Whatever can this mean?" she whispered to herself.

They all sat looking silently at the fire. They were the Twelve Months of the Year. The great Setchéne, January, sat higher than the others; his hair and moustache were as white as snow, and in his hand he held a wand. Marouckla was terribly frightened at first, but she took several deep breaths and her courage returned. She drew nearer the fire and said, "My dear people, may I warm myself at your fire? I am chilled through by the winter cold."

The great Setchéne raised his head and asked, "What brings you here, my child? What is it that you seek?"

"I am looking for violets," replied the maiden, feeling rather foolish.

The Setchéne raised his eyebrows in surprise. "This is not the season for violets! Look around you, Girl, don't you see the snow covering the ground?"

"I know," sighed Marouckla, "but my sister Helen and my stepmother have ordered me to bring them some violets from your mountain. If I don't they will kill me."

The great Setchéne studied the girl for a moment in silence, and then he turned to March, the youngest of the months, and pressed the wand into his hand. "Brother Brezéne, take the highest seat."

Brezéne obeyed, and as he took his seat he waved the wand over the fire. Immediately the flames leaped and rose toward the sky, the snow began to melt and the trees and shrubs to bud; the grass became green, and from between its blades peeped pale primrose. It was Spring, and the meadows were blue with violets.

"Gather them quickly, Marouckla," urged Brezéne.

Joyfully she hurried to pick the flowers, and her basket was soon overflowing with them. She thanked the Twelve Months, and ran home as fast as her legs could carry her. As she burst through the cottage door her stepmother shouted, "Marouckla! I thought I told you not to come back unless you . . . unless . . . what?!" Her eyes widened in amazement as she caught sight of the violets.

"Wherever did you find them, Marouckla?" Helen demanded angrily.

"Under the trees on the mountain slope," said Marouckla. "You act surprised, dear sister. Didn't you ask for violets?"

Helen snatched the flowers from her sister and took them to her room, not even thanking Marouckla for the trouble she had taken.

The next day she came to breakfast with a sly smile

on her face. "Marouckla," she said sweetly, "fetch me some strawberries from the forest. Remember they must be sweet and ripe."

"Strawberries?" exclaimed Marouckla. "Who has ever heard of strawberries ripening in the snow?"

"Hold your tongue, you little worm! How dare you speak to me so! If you don't bring me my strawberries, I will kill you!"

The stepmother grabbed Marouckla by the hair and shoved her out the door, bolting it behind her. The unhappy girl made her way back toward the mountain and to the large fire around which sat the Twelve Months. The great Setchéne was again occupying the highest place.

"My dear friends," Marouckla smiled, "may I please warm myself at your fire? The winter chill is worse than ever it was before."

The great Setchéne raised his head. "Why are you here, Marouckla? What is it you seek?"

"Strawberries," replied Marouckla, "my sister has sent me out to gather strawberries."

"We are in the middle of winter," replied Setchéne with a shake of his head, "and you must realize that strawberries do not grow in the snow."

"I know, I know," said Marouckla. "But if I return without any strawberries, my sister has vowed to kill me. Pray, good people, tell me where I can find them!"

The great Setchéne rose and crossed over to the month directly opposite him. He placed the wand in her hand and said, "Sister Tchervéne, please take my place in the highest seat."

June obeyed, and as she waved the wand over the fire, the flames leapt toward the sky. Instantly the snow melted, the earth was covered with green plants, trees were cloaked in leaves, birds began to sing, and various flowers bloomed throughout the forest. It was Summer in all her glory. Under the bushes masses of star-shaped flowers changed into ripening strawberries. Before Marouckla's startled eyes they quickly covered the glade, looking like a carpet of red.

"Gather them quickly, Marouckla," said Tchervéne.

Happily she thanked the Twelve Months, and having filled her apron, ran speedily home. Helen and her mother stared at the strawberries which filled the cottage with their delicious fragrance.

"Where did you find them, Marouckla?" Helen demanded crossly.

"Right up on the mountain, where you told me to go. Are they not to your satisfaction?"

Helen gave a few to her mother, and gobbled the rest down herself; not one did she offer her stepsister. The next morning she took a fancy to having some red, ripe apples.

"Run, Marouckla, run into the forest and fetch me the freshest apples you can find."

"Apples in winter? You must be kidding! Why, the trees have neither leaves nor fruit."

"Idle wench, go this minute," said Helen. "Unless you bring back apples we will kill you."

As had happened twice before, the stepmother seized Marouckla roughly and turned her out of the house. The poor child went weeping up the mountain, across the deep snow upon which lay no human footprint, and on toward the fire around which were the Twelve Months. Motionless they sat, and on the highest stone was the great Setchéne. They had helped her before, would they help her again?

"My good people, may I warm myself at your fire?" Marouckla asked as she drew near. "The winter winds chill me so."

The great Setchéne raised his head and looked directly at the girl. "Why are you again here, my child? What is it you seek now?"

"I am here to look for red apples," replied Marouckla.

"This is winter, my girl, and not the season for red apples," observed the great Setchéne with a smile.

"I know," answered the girl, "but my sister and stepmother sent me to fetch red apples from the mountain; if I return without them they will kill me."

The great Setchéne rose and went over to one of elderly months, to whom he handed the wand and said, "My brother Zaré, do take the highest seat."

September moved to the highest stone and waved his wand over the fire. There was a flare of red flames, the snow disappeared, but the fading leaves which trembled on the trees were sent by a cold northeast wind in yellow masses to the glade. Only a few flowers of autumn were visible, such as the fleabane and the red gillyflower, and there were colchi cums in the ravine, and northern heather under the beech trees. At first Marouckla looked in vain for red apples. Then she spotted a tree which grew to a great height, and from the branches hung the bright red fruit. "Quickly, Marouckla, pick the apples," urged Zaré. The girl was delighted and shook the tree. First one apple fell, and then another.

"That is enough," said Zaré. "Hurry home now."

Thanking the Months, she returned home. Helen was speechless and the widow stared at the fruit in wonder.

"Where did you gather them?" asked the stepmother.

"From the mountaintop. There are many up there."

"Then why did you not bring more?" Helen sputtered angrily. "You must have eaten them on the way back, you wicked girl!"

"Oh, no! I never even tasted them!" said Marouckla. "I shook the tree twice, and a single apple fell each time. I was not allowed to shake it again, but was told to go home!"

"May Zeus strike you with his thunderbolt!" shrieked Helen, striking her repeatedly.

Marouckla prayed to die rather than suffer anymore mistreatment. Crying bitterly, she ran into the kitchen. Helen and her mother each had an apple, and found them more delicious than any they had tasted before.

"Listen, Mother," said Helen, "fetch my cloak. I will gather more apples myself. These are too good to leave in the forest! I will be able to find the mountain and the tree, and nobody will dare to tell me to stop shaking the apples down!"

Despite her mother's worries, Helen put on her cloak, covered her head with a warm hood, and took the road to the mountain. The mother stood in the doorway and watched as her daughter disappeared into the distance.

Snow covered everything, and not a single footprint was seen on the surface. Helen lost her way, and wandered here and there. After a long while she saw a light above her, and following it she reached the mountaintop. There was the flaming fire, there were the twelve blocks of stone, and the Twelve Months. At first she was frightened and hesitated, then she came nearer and warmed her hands. She did not ask permission, nor did she speak one polite word.

"What has brought you here, Helen?" said the great Setchéne severely. "What is it you seek?"

"I am not obliged to tell you, Old Man. What business is it of yours?" she replied disdainfully, turning her back on the fire and going toward the forest.

The great Setchéne frowned, and waved his wand over his head. Instantly the sky was covered with clouds, the fire went low, snow fell in large flakes, and an icy wind howled round the mountain. Amid the fury of the storm Helen cursed her stepsister. Her cloak failed to warm her frozen limbs, and she became lost among the swirling drifts.

The stepmother kept on waiting for her daughter to return. She looked out from the window and watched from the doorstep, but her daughter never appeared. The hours passed slowly, and the storm grew worse, but Helen did not return.

"Can it be that the apples have charmed her away from her home? Perhaps my selfish daughter has decided to keep them all to herself!" the old woman grumbled. Then she clad herself in hood and cloak and went in search of her daughter. "When I get my hands on that girl, I'll shake her soundly for causing me such worry!" Snow fell in huge flakes; it covered everything; it lay untouched by human footsteps. For a long time the old woman wandered here and there, the icy northeast wind whistled in the mountains, but no voice answered her cries.

Day after day Marouckla worked and prayed, and waited; but neither her stepmother nor her sister returned, and she could only suspect that they had been frozen to death on the mountain. The inheritance of a small house, a field and a cow fell to Marouckla. In the course of time an honest farmer came to share them with her, and their lives were ever after happy and peaceful.

Prince Slugobyl
and the Invisible Knight

Once there was a king who had many daughters and only one son, and his name was Prince Slugobyl. There was nothing that the young prince loved more than to travel, and when he reached his twenty-first birthday he begged his father to let him go on a journey. At first the king refused—there was no way he would ever let his son leave—but the prince gave him no rest until he agreed to let him wander the world over.

"So many beautiful and strange things will I see!" the prince exclaimed. "The adventures I'll undergo! The happiness, knowledge and wisdom I will attain! You will not regret letting me go, Father, for I'll return to you a better man."

"Not so fast, Slugobyl," cautioned the king. "In view of your young years, I am sending along a servant, one who is my most faithful and honest man, and who is experienced in the ways of the world." The young prince was too happy to argue the matter, and when all was ready, he bade his father and sisters good-bye and set off with his servant to visit the lands of his dreams.

As Prince Slugobyl was trotting along, letting his horse set its own pace, he saw a beautiful white swan pursued by an eagle. The eagle was about to seize the swan in its talons when the prince grabbed his crossbow and shot the eagle from the sky. The rescued swan stopped in its flight, and flew to land before the prince's feet. "Prince Slugobyl," the bird whistled, "it is not a mere swan who you saved, and who thanks you for your help, but the daughter of the Invisible Knight. To escape the pursuit of the giant Kostey, I changed myself into a swan. He pursued me as an eagle. My father will gladly be in service to you, in return for this kindness to me. When in need of help,

you only have to say three times, 'Invisible Knight, come to me.'"

Having thus spoken, the swan rose on snowy wings and flew away. The prince watched as she faded from view, and then he continued his journey. He traveled far, and farther than far, over high mountains, through dark forests, across barren deserts, and so on until he arrived in the middle of a vast plain where every green thing had been burned up by the rays of the sun. Not a single tree or bush or plant of any kind was to be found. No bird was heard to sing, no insect to hum, no breath of air to stir the stillness of this desolate land.

Having ridden a good many hours, the prince was terribly thirsty, and he sent his servant to seek a well or a spring. He searched in the opposite direction. They soon found a well of cool, fresh water but, unluckily enough, it was without a bucket or rope.

"Take the leather straps used for tethering our horses, put it round your body, and I will lower you in the well," the prince said to his servant. "I don't think I can endure this thirst any longer."

"Your Highness," said the servant humbly, "I am far heavier than you, and you are not as strong as I am. I do not think you will be able to pull me out of the water. Therefore, if you will go down first, I shall be able to pull you up when you have quenched your thirst."

The prince considered this, and fastened an end of the strap under his arms. "All right, lower away!" he said cheerfully. The servant let him down easily, and there the prince drank deeply of the clear, cold water. He ruled a flask for the servant, then called, "Okay, pull me up, I'm ready!"

"You are, are you?" said the servant from the top of the well. "Listen, Slugobyl, from the day you were born you have never known anything but luxury, pleasure, and happiness; as for myself, I have only known poverty. Your father is a skinflint, and the servants are little better than slaves!"

"What are you saying?" asked Slugobyl nervously.

"I'm saying this. We will now change places, and you shall be my servant. If you refuse, you might as well make your peace with God now, for you can be sure that I won't be pulling you back up."

"You would be so wicked as to murder me?" the prince asked incredulously. "No good could ever come from such an action. You know what dreadful punishment awaits a murderer; your hands will be plunged into boiling tar, your shoulders will be bruised with blows from red-hot iron clubs, and your neck will be sawn with a wooden saw."

"Bold words for one at the end of his rope," sneered the servant. "Go ahead and beat me all you want in the next world, but in this world I shall drown you." He let the strap slide through his fingers.

"All right!" shouted the prince.

"All right what?" called the servant, grabbing the strap at the last possible second.

"All right! I accept your terms. You shall be the prince and I will be your servant. I give you my word."

"Words! What good are words? I have no faith in words that are carried away by the first wind that blows. Swear that you will uphold your promise in writing."

"I swear it," said the prince. "Now let me up!"

"Not quite yet," said the servant. He let down a paper and pencil, and dictated the following: *'I hereby declare that I renounce my name and rights in favor of the bearer of this writing, and I acknowledge him to be my prince, and that I am his servant.'*

"Now sign it!" cried the servant. "Sign it now!"

Gritting his teeth, the prince wrote: *"signed from the bottom of a well, Prince Slugobyl."*

The servant clutched the document, which you must know he was quite unable to read, pulled up the prince, and forced him to exchange clothes. Thus disguised, they traveled on for another week, and at last arrived at a large city, where they went straight to the king's palace. There the false prince dismissed his "servant" to the stables, and presented himself before the king. "I have come to demand the hand of your wise and beautiful daughter," he proclaimed in a rather haughty voice. "Her fame has reached my father's court, and he is willing to offer an alliance should I be allowed to marry her. If not, I can only promise you war."

"Prayers and threats are equally out of place," answered the king. "Nevertheless, Prince, as proof of the esteem in which I regard your father, I will grant your request. But on one condition: you must save us from a large army that even now approaches our town. Do this, and my daughter shall be yours."

"Easier done than said," said the imposter. "I can quickly get rid of them, however near they may be. I swear that by tomorrow morning I will have freed the land from them entirely."

In the evening the phony prince went to the stables and, calling his pretended servant, saluted him respectfully and said, "Listen, my dear old friend, I want you to go immediately outside the town and destroy the army that is besieging us. But you must do it in such a way that everyone will believe that I have done it. In exchange for this tiny little favor, I promise to return the writing in which you renounced your title to me."

"You want me to defeat an entire army by myself?" the prince asked.

"Do it, or I will expose you for a traitor," threatened the imposter.

The real prince put on his armor, mounted his horse, and rode outside the city gates. There he stopped and called out "Invisible Knight! Invisible Knight! Invisible Knight, come to me now."

"I am here, my prince," said a voice close to his side. The prince looked all around but he could not see anybody. "I will do anything you wish," the voice continued. "You saved my daughter from the hands of the giant Kostey, and I shall always be grateful."

Slugobyl showed him the army he had to destroy by morning, and the Invisible Knight chuckled. "Is that all?" he asked. "Simple enough." Then he sang a little tune:

"Magu, Horse with Golden Mane,
I want your help yet once again,
Walk not the earth but fly through space
as lightnings flash or thunders race.
Swift as the arrow from the bow,
come quick, yet so that none will know."

Suddenly a magnificent grey horse appeared from a whirl-wind of smoke, and from his proud head hung a blazing gold mane. Swift as the wind he was; flames of fire shot forth from his nostrils, lightning flashed from his eyes, and smoke poured from his ears. The Invisible Knight leaped upon his back and called to the prince, "Take my sword and destroy the left wing of the army, and I will take the right wing and the center units."

The two heroes charged into battle and attacked the invaders with such a fury that on all sides men fell like chopped wood or dried grass. A frightful massacre followed, and it was in vain that the army fled, for the two knights seemed to be everywhere at once. Within a very short time only the dead and dying remained on the battlefield, and the two conquerers returned to the village. On reaching the palace steps, the Invisible Knight melted in the morning mist, and it was several more steps before the serving-man prince realized he was alone. Silently he returned to the stables.

That same night it had happened that the king's daughter could not sleep, and had remained on her balcony where she witnessed all that had taken place. She had overheard the conversation between the imposter and the real prince, had seen the prince call for the Invisible Knight, had seen the arrival of the magnificent stallion, and had seen the hero rush forward to the attack. She had seen and understood everything, but she determined to keep it to herself a while longer.

When morning came the king, her father, celebrated the victory of the false prince with great rejoicing. He loaded the dishonorable man with honors and presents, then called his daughter to his side. "It is my wish that you marry this worthy young man," her father beamed.

The princess could keep silent no longer. She approached the real prince, who was seated at a table with the other servants, took him by the arm and led him to the king. "Father, this is the man who has saved our country from the enemy, this is the man whom God has destined to be my husband."

"What is this?" the king interrupted. "What are you blathering about, Girl?"

"The man to whom you pay honor is but an imposter, one who has robbed his master of his name and rights. Last night I witnessed deeds which no eye has ever seen and no ear has ever heard, but which I shall reveal to you now. Demand that this traitor show you the writing which proves the truth of what I say."

Smugly, the false prince swaggered up to the king. It did not matter if he was once a servant, he now had the paper that proved the real prince had given up all his rights. The king read the paper aloud,

"The bearer of this document, the false and wicked servant of the serving-man prince, shall receive the punishment his sin deserves.

Signed from the bottom of a well, Prince Slugobyl"

"What?" the traitor shrieked. "Is that what the paper says?"

"Foolish man," said Prince Slugobyl, "it's a pity that you never learned to read."

The poor wretched man threw himself at the feet of the king and begged for mercy, but he received his punishment: he was tied to the tails of four wild horses and torn to pieces.

Prince Slugobyl married the princess. The Invisible Knight served as the best man, and the Swan-Girl as the maid of honor. Oh, it was a grand wedding! I myself was there, and drank of the mead and the wine, but you can be sure that I did not let it go to my head.

The Lost Child

Long, long ago there lived a very rich nobleman; but though he had more wealth than most men dare dream of, he was not happy. He had no children to whom he could leave his gold. He was, besides, no longer young, and neither was his wife. Every morning they went to church to pray for a son.

At last, after they had waited many years, God sent them what their hearts desired most. The night before the child was born, the nobleman had a very strange dream: the boy's only chance of living would depend upon one condition, that his feet never touched the earth until he was twelve years old.

Was this a true dream? The father dared not take any chances. Great care was taken that the evil prophecy would be avoided at all costs; only the most trustworthy of nurses were hired to look after the boy. As the years passed the child was never left alone. Sometimes he was carried in his nurses' arms, sometimes he was rocked in his cradle, but never once did his feet touch the ground.

When the boy's twelfth birthday approached, the father began preparations for a magnificent feast which would be given to celebrate his son's release. On the final day before the curse's end, a horrible noise shook the castle; screams, howls and yowls issued from the walls as the floor boards trembled and shook. In her terror the nurse dropped the child and ran to look out the window. That very instant the noise and the shaking stopped. Turning to pick up the boy, she screamed when she discovered he was not there. Only then did the poor nurse remember that she had disobeyed her master's orders.

Hearing her cries and lamentations, the other servants of the castle ran to her aid. "What is it?" they asked. "What is the matter?" The nurse could only wail and point to the empty spot on the floor.

The father entered the room. Quickly glancing from one horrified face to another, he grabbed the nurse and shook her by the shoulders. "What has happened here?" he demanded. "Where is my son?" The nurse, trembling and weeping, told of the disappearance of his son, his only child. No words can describe the anguish in the father's heart! He sent servants to search every corner of the castle, but despite many hours of hunting through closets and under beds and behind drapes, they could not find him. The nobleman and his wife gave orders, they begged and prayed, they threw away money right and left, they promised everything if only their son might be returned to them. No trace of him could ever be found. He had vanished as completely as if he had never existed.

It was a great many years later that the unhappy couple learned that in one of the most beautiful rooms of their castle were heard footsteps, as if someone were walking up and down, and dismal groans at every midnight. Anxious to follow the matter up, for there was a slight chance it might in some way concern their lost son, the nobleman made it known that a reward of three hundred gold pieces would be given to anyone who would watch for one whole night in the haunted room. Many were willing, but not one had the courage to stay till the end; for at midnight, when the dismal groans were heard, they would run away rather than risk their lives for a measly pile of gold. The poor father and mother were in despair. How could they discover the truth of this dark mystery?

Close to the castle dwelt a widow, a miller by trade, who had three daughters. They were very poor, and hardly earned enough for their daily needs. When word reached them of the midnight noises in the castle, the oldest daughter said, "We are so very poor that we have nothing to lose if we try for the reward. Surely we might be able to earn those three hundred gold pieces. So much money for one night's work! I should like to try, Mother, if you will let me."

The old woman shrugged her shoulders. She hardly knew what to say, but when she thought of their poverty and the difficulty they had in earning a living, she gave permission to her eldest daughter to remain one night in the haunted room. The daughter went to ask the nobleman's consent.

"You are the first woman who has asked to stay in the room," the nobleman said. "Do you really have the courage to watch for a whole night in a place you know is haunted? Are you sure you're not afraid?"

"I am willing to try this very night," she answered confidently. "I would only ask you to give me some food to cook for my supper, for I am very hungry."

Orders were given that the miller's oldest daughter should be supplied with everything she wanted. Indeed, she was given so much food that she had enough for three meals. With the food, some dry firewood and a candle, she entered the haunted room. She first lit the fire and put on her saucepans, then she laid the table and made the bed. This filled up the early part of the evening. The time passed so quickly that she was surprised to hear the clock strike midnight, and at the last stroke, footsteps shook the room and dismal groans filled the air. The frightened girl ran from one corner to the other, but could not see anyone. But the footsteps and the groans did not stop. Suddenly, a young man appeared from the shadows and asked, "Who did you cook this food for?"

"For myself," the girl said.

The gentle face of the stranger grew sad, and after a short silence he asked again, "This table, who did you set this table for?"

"For myself," she repeated.

The brow of the young man clouded over, and the beautiful blue eyes filled with tears as he asked a final question, "And this bed, who did you make this bed for?"

"For myself," she said in the same selfish and indifferent tone of voice. Who was this person anyway?

Tears fell from the young man's eyes as he waved his arms in the air and vanished.

The next morning she told the nobleman all that had happened, but without mentioning the painful impression her answers had made upon the stranger. The three hundred golden crowns were paid, and the father was thankful to have at last heard something that might possibly lead to the return of his son. Surely this strange young man must be his child!

The nobleman posted another three hundred gold crowns for the one who could gather any new information. The second daughter of the widow, having been told by her sister what to do and how to answer the stranger, went to the castle to offer her services. The nobleman willingly agreed, and orders were given that she should be provided with everything she might want. Without another moment lost, the middle daughter entered the haunted room, lit the fire, put on the saucepans, spread a clean white cloth upon the table, made the bed, and awaited the hour of midnight. When the young stranger stepped from the shadows he asked, "Who did you make this food for? Who did you set the table for? Who did you make the bed for?"

The girl answered as her sister told her to, "For me, for myself alone."

As on the night before, the man burst into tears, waved his arms, and suddenly disappeared.

Next morning she told the nobleman all that had happened, including the sad impression her answers gave the stranger. The three hundred gold pieces were given to her, and she went home happily, without another thought of the tortured soul she met the night before.

On the third day word reached the widow and her daughters that the king offered another three hundred gold crowns for the one who could bring his son home. The youngest daughter wished to try her luck. "Sisters," she said, "you each succeeded in earning three hundred gold crowns. I too would like to earn some money to help out our mother. I will spend a night in the haunted room."

The widow loved her youngest daughter more dearly than the others, and dreaded sending her into any danger; but as the elder ones had been so successful, she allowed the fair young woman to take the same chance. So with the instructions from her sisters as to what she should say and do, and with the nobleman's consent and abundant provisions, the youngest daughter entered the haunted room. Having lit the fire, put on the saucepans, laid the table and made the bed, she awaited with hope and fear for the hour of midnight.

As twelve o'clock struck, the room was shaken by the footsteps of someone who walked up and down, and the air was filled with all sorts of cries and groans. The girl looked everywhere, but no living thing could be seen. Suddenly there stood before her a young man who asked in a gentle voice, "For whom did you prepare this food?"

Her sisters had told her how to answer and how to act, but when she looked into the sad eyes of the stranger she resolved to treat him more kindly.

"Well, you do not answer me," the young man said. "For whom is the food prepared?"

Somewhat confused, she said, "I-I prepared it for myself, but you are welcome to eat it if you want."

At these words the stranger looked less tense, and a smile began to form. "And this table? Who did you set it for?"

"For myself, unless you would do me the honor of being my guest."

A bright smile illumined his face, making his blue eyes twinkle. "And this bed, for whom did you make it?"

"For myself, but if you are tired you may rest on it."

The man clapped his hands together for joy and replied, "Ah, that's right! I accept your kind invitation with pleasure. But wait, I beg that you wait for me a moment, I must first thank my friends for the care they have given me."

A fresh warm breath of spring filled the air, while at the same moment a deep precipice opened in the middle of the floor. He stepped lightly into it and she, anxious to see what would happen, followed him, holding onto his mantle. Thus they both reached the bottom of the precipice. Down there a new world opened itself to her eyes. To the right flowed a river of liquid gold, to the left rose high mountains of solid gold, in the center lay a large meadow covered with millions of flowers. The stranger went on, and the girl followed unnoticed. As the young man went he saluted the field flowers as if they were old friends, stroking them and leaving them with regret. They came to a forest where the trees were made of gold; birds of different kinds perched familiarly on his head and shoulders. He spoke to and petted each one. While the young man was thus engaged, the girl broke off a branch from one of the golden trees and hid it in remembrance of this strange land.

Leaving the forest of gold, they reached a wood where all the trees were of silver. Their arrival was greeted by an immense number of animals of various kinds. These crowded together and pushed one against another to get close to their friend. He spoke to each one and stroked and petted them. Meanwhile, the girl broke off a branch of silver from one of the trees, saying to herself, "These will serve me as tokens of this wonderful land, for my sisters would not believe me if I only told them of it."

When the young stranger had taken leave of all his friends, he returned by the paths he had come, and the girl followed him, still unseen. Arriving at the foot of the precipice, the young man began to ascend, and the girl followed silently, holding onto his mantle so she would not get lost. Up they went, higher and higher, until they reached the room in the castle. The floor closed up without a trace of the opening. The girl returned to her place by the fire.

"All of my farewells have been spoken," the prince said. "Now we can have supper."

The beautiful young woman hurried to place upon the table the food she had prepared, and sitting side by side they supped together. When they had filled themselves with the fine food he said, "Now it is time to rest."

He lay down on the carefully made bed and in a few moments was sleeping peacefully. The girl placed by his side the gold and silver branches she had picked up in the Mineral Land.

The next day the sun was already high in the sky, and as yet the girl had not come to give the nobleman an account of herself. He grew impatient. He waited and waited, becoming more and more uneasy. What had happened to the girl? At last he determined to go and see for himself what had happened. Picture for yourself his surprise and joy when, on entering the haunted chamber, he saw his long-lost son sleeping on the bed, while beside him sat the widow's beautiful daughter. At that moment the son awoke. The father, overwhelmed with joy, summoned all the attendants of the castle to rejoice with him in his newfound happiness.

Then the young man saw the miller's daughter and the two branches of metal, and said with astonishment, "What is this I see? Did you then follow me down there? Know that by this brave act you have broken the spell and released me from the enchantment of the Mineral King. These two branches will make two palaces for our future dwelling."

Thereupon he took the branches and threw them out the window. From one branch sprang a castle of gold, from the other a castle of silver. There they lived happily as man and wife, the nobleman's son and the miller's daughter, and if they are not dead they live there still.

The Lazy Brother

On the banks of the river, where there was always good fishing, lived an old widower with his three sons. The two older boys were clever, smart, hard-working young men, both already married; the youngest was lazy and stupid, and still a bachelor. The father thought this son would never find a bride! When the old man was dying, he called his children to him and told them how he wanted to leave his property. Each son would receive three hundred florins inheritance, and the house would go to the two married sons. After the father's death, he was buried with great ceremony, and a splendid feast was given for all his friends and relatives; all of these honors were supposed to benefit the man's soul.

When the older brothers took possession of their inheritance, they said to the youngest, "Listen, I think it's best that you give us your share of the money, too. We intend to go into the world as merchants, and when we make a great deal of money we will buy you a hat, a sash, and a brand new pair of red boots. What do you say?"

"I say that sounds wonderful!" grinned the younger brother. For a long time the silly fellow had wanted a cap, a sash, and a pair of red boots. He was easily persuaded to give up his money.

"Good," said the middle brother. "You will be better off here at home. Just remember to mind what your sisters-in-law tell you."

The brothers set out on their journey, and crossed the sea in search of fortune. The fool of the family remained at home and, as he was an out-and-out sluggard, he would lie for whole days at a time on the warm stove without doing a lick of work, and only obeyed his sisters-in-law when they threatened to beat him or withhold his food. He liked fried onions, potato soup, and cider better than anything else in the world, and would do almost anything to get them.

One day his sisters-in-law asked him to fetch them some water.

The fool glanced out the window. "It's the middle of winter and it's freezing out there. Go yourselves. I prefer to stay here by the fire."

"Stupid, stupid boy!" one of them snapped as she struck him with her ladle. "We will have onions, potato soup, and cider ready for you when you come back. If you refuse to do what we ask you we shall tell our husbands!"

"Right!" the other woman chimed in. "And when they find out how you've misbehaved there will be neither cap, nor sash, nor red boots for you!"

"All right, all right! I'll go!" the lazy brother grumbled as he rolled off the stove, took a hatchet and a couple of pails, and went down to the river. On the surface of the water, where the ice had been broken, was a large pike. The man seized him by the fins and hauled him out.

"If you will let me go," begged the pike, "I promise to give you everything you wish for."

"You, a fish, can promise me that?"

"Certainly!"

"Well, I guess I would like all of my desires to be fulfilled the moment I utter them."

"You shall have everything you want the moment you say these words:

'At my request, and by orders of the pike,
may such and such things happen, as I like.'"

"It's that simple?" asked the fool. "Just wait a moment while I try this out.

"At my request, and by orders of the pike,
bring onions, cider, and soup, just as I like."

That very moment his favorite dishes appeared before him. He stuffed himself till he could eat no more, then said, "Very good, very good, indeed! But will it always be the same?"

"Always," said the pike. "Now can you return me to the water? I'm feeling rather parched."

The lazy man put the pike back into the river, and turning toward the buckets, said:

"At my request, and by orders of the pike,
walk home by yourselves, my pails—that I should like."

The buckets and the strong rod they were fastened to immediately set off and walked solemnly along, the lazy man following them with his hands in his pockets and whistling a tune.

When they reached the house, he put the buckets in their places, and again stretched himself out to enjoy the warmth of the stove. His sisters-in-law entered the room and said, "Come and chop some wood for us."

"You mean now?" asked the man.

"Right now!"

"Bother! Do it yourselves."

"But it is not fit work for women," one of them protested. "Besides, if you don't do it the stove will grow cold, and then you will be the one to suffer! Now what do you think of that?"

"Yeah, and no red boots!" said the other. The lazy man sat up and said:

"At my request, and by orders of the pike,
let what my sisters want be done—that's what I like."

Instantly the hatchet came out from behind a stool and chopped up a large heap of wood, put a part of it on the stove, and retired to its corner. All this time the sluggard was snoring away by the stove, and the sisters-in-law were staring in open-mouthed wonder.

The next day wood had to be cut from the forest. The lazy man thought he would like to show off in front of his neighbors, so he pulled a sledge out of the shed, loaded it with onions and soup, and said some magic words.

The sledge started off in a flash, and passed through the village at a rattling pace, ran over several people, and frightened the children so that they ran crying home to their mothers.

When the forest was reached, the lazy man looked on, eating his soup and onions, while the blocks of woods were cut, tied, and laid in the sledge as if by invisible hands. On the return trip through the village the men who had been hurt or frightened earlier in the morning seized hold of the sluggard and yanked him off his sledge. They dragged him along by the hair and gave him a sound thrashing.

"Ow! Stop!" cried the sluggard. "Stop, I say!" When he realized they would not he said:

"At my request, and by orders of the pike,
come, logs, haste, and my assailants strike!"

In a moment all the blocks of wood jumped off the sledge and began to hit right and left, scattering the men in all directions.

The lazy man laughed at them till his sides ached. Then he hopped up on his sledge and within the hour was again lying comfortably on his stove.

From that day on he became famous, and his doings were talked about in every farm and village throughout the countryside. At last word reached the king, whose curiosity prompted him to send out soldiers to retrieve the man.

The soldiers burst into the little farm kitchen, and the chief of them shouted, "Hey, you! Come down off that stove and follow us to the king's palace."

"Why should I? Does he have better cider, onions, and soup than I have here at home?"

"What insolence! Come off that stove before I drag you off."

"I'd like to see you try!"

"Oh you would, would you?"

The sluggard grinned and said,

"At my request, and by orders of the pike,
may this man get a taste of what a broom is like."

A large broom, one not too particularly clean, immediately hopped up, dipped itself in a pail of water, and brushed the soldier's teeth. He had to jump out of a window to escape, spitting out straws all the way back to the palace. The king, amazed at the lazy man's refusal to come, sent another troop of soldiers.

The leader of this troop was more polite than the last, and he went up to the sluggard and said, "Good day, my friend! Will you come with me to see the king? He has heard of your desires, and wishes to present you with a cap, a waistband, and a pair of red boots."

"Sure, I'll come over," said the lazy man. "Go on ahead, I'll soon overtake you."

Then he ate as much as he could hold of his favorite dishes and went to sleep on the stove. He slept so long that his sisters-in-law had to shake him awake. "You'll be late if you don't leave at once!" they cried. The lazy man yawned and then said:

"At my request, and by orders of the pike,
this stove to carry me before the king I'd like."

Hardly had he said these words aloud when the stove detached itself and carried him right to the palace door. The king and all his courtiers were filled with awe, and they ran about like hens.

"I have come to fetch the hat, belt, and boots you promised me," the lazy man said.

The Princess Gapiomila came down the stairs to find out what the commotion was about. The sluggard looked at her, and never had he seen a more beautiful woman in all his life. Under his breath he whispered:

"At my request, and by orders of the pike,
that this princess may love me—that I should like!"

Then he ordered the stove to take him back home, and when he got there he continued to eat onions and soup and to drink cider. "This is the life!" he exclaimed.

The princess had, of course, fallen in love with him—but it was love at first sight, and not because the sluggard wished it. She begged her father to send for him again. "This time ask him to stay longer," she suggested.

The sluggard would not consent, and the king had him bound when asleep, and dragged to the palace. He then called one of his most celebrated magicians to come forward and fashion a crystal cask.

"A crystal cask?" the princess asked. "Whatever do you want that for?"

"Just a little test, my dear," the king murmured. "Don't worry your pretty little head over it."

"Father . . ." she began indignantly.

The king ordered that the princess and the sluggard should be shut in the crystal cask. Then he had a great balloon filled with gas attached to the cask, and sent it up in the air among the clouds. The princess cried bitterly, but the fool sat still and said he felt quite comfortable. "I bet I'm the first in my family who has ever flown like a bird!" he said cheerfully. At last the princess persuaded him to use his powers, and he said:

"At my request, and by orders of the pike,
this cask of crystal at once must strike
upon a friendly island—this I should like."

The crystal cask descended, and landed on a hospitable island where they could have all they wanted simply by wishing for it. The princess and her friend walked about, eating when hungry, drinking when thirsty, and sleeping when tired. The sluggard was very happy and content—what more could he possibly wish for? But the lady begged him to create a palace. "I'm tired of sleeping in the open."

A palace rose out of the ground before them. It was built of white marble, with crystal windows, a roof of yellow amber, and golden furniture. The lady was absolutely delighted with it!

The next day the princess wanted a good road made, "Along which I may go to see my father."

A fairy-like bridge stretched across the waters, connecting the island with her father's kingdom. It was made of crystal, and had gold balustrades set with diamonds. There was not another bridge like it anywhere. "Let's go see my father at once!" the princess said.

The sluggard was about to accompany the princess across the bridge when he suddenly remembered his own appearance. Blushing with embarrassment he looked down at himself. "What an awkward, stupid fellow I look!" he sighed.

"I can't be seen walking beside such a lovely and graceful creature.

"At my request, and by orders of the pike,
to be both handsome, wise and clever—
that I should like."

The sluggard suddenly became as handsome, wise and as clever as it was possible to be. Then he climbed into a carriage beside Gapiomila, and they drove across the bridge that led to the king's palace.

The king smiled when he saw them, and gave them both his blessing so that they could be married that very evening. A great many guests were invited to the wedding feast; I, too, was there and drank freely of wine and hydromel—perhaps a little too freely because I had a tremendous headache the next day!

The Broad Man,
the Tall Man, and the
Man with Eyes of Flame

This tale happened in the days when cats wore shoes, when frogs croaked in grandmothers' chairs, when donkeys clanked their spurs on the pavements like bold knights, and when rabbits chased dogs. You can see that it must have been a very, very long time ago!

In those days the king of a certain country had a daughter who was not only beautiful and charming, but also quite intelligent. Many kings, princes and nobles traveled to the kingdom, each hoping to make the maiden his wife. But she was not interested in any of them. Finally, it was announced that the princess would marry the man who for three successive nights should keep such strict watch upon her that she could not escape unnoticed, thus proving his intelligence was at least as great as hers. Those who failed were to have their heads cut off. She thought that by having such terms the suitors would go away and leave her in peace, but such was not the case.

The news of this challenge was spoken about in all parts of the world. A great many men hurried to make the trial, each taking a turn at keeping watch, and it was the last thing he would ever do. Not one of them could prevent the princess's escape, let alone be able to tell how she did it. The heads of the losers were set on pikes along the road to the palace, a deterrent to all other challengers.

Now it so happened that Matthias, prince of a royal city, heard of what was going on and determined that he was the one who could watch her all three nights. He was young, handsome, and clever, and brave as an eagle. His father begged him not to go, using prayers and threats, and finally resorted to begging. "You are my only son and heir. Who will rule the kingdom if you fail?" What can a poor father do? Feeling broken and worn out, he was at last forced to give his consent. Matthias filled his purse with many a gold coin, tied a well-proven sword to his side, and set off alone to seek his fortune.

Walking along the next day, he met a man who seemed barely able to walk, dragging one leg after the other. "Where are you going, Grandfather?" Matthias asked.

"I am traveling the world over in search of happiness," said the man, not pausing in his efforts.

"What is your profession?"

"I have no profession," the man glanced briefly at Matthias, "but I can do what no one else can. I am called Broad, because I have the power of increasing the size of my body so that there is room for a whole regiment of soldiers inside me."

"Really?" laughed Matthias. "I have never heard of such a thing!"

"You don't believe me? Then watch." So saying, he puffed himself out until he formed a wall from one side of the road to the other.

"Bravo!" cried Matthias. "I apologize for having doubted you. Would you care to travel with me? I, too, am traveling across the world in search of happiness."

"If there is nothing bad in it, I am willing," answered Broad.

A little ways on they met a very slender man, frightfully skinny, and tall and straight as a pine tree. "Where are you going, good man?" asked Matthias, filled with curiosity.

"I am traveling about the world, I'm going no place in particular."

"What is your profession?"

"Profession? I have none. But I know something every one else is ignorant of."

"Oh?" asked Broad. "What is that?"

"I am called Tall, a name that well suits me. Without leaving the earth I can stretch out and touch the clouds. When I walk I can clear a mile at each step."

"That is impressive, indeed," said Prince Matthias, having learned to respect such claims. Without further prompting Tall stretched himself until his head was lost in the clouds, while his feet, which never left the earth, cleared a mile at each step.

When they caught up with him again, Matthias said, "I like that, my good friend. Come, would you travel with us?"

"I have nothing better at the moment, why not?"

So they continued on their way together. As they paced through a forest they saw a man placing the trunks of trees one upon another.

"What are you trying to do there?" Broad called out to him.

"I have Eyes of Flame," said the ordinary-looking man. "I am building a pile here for a little morning workout." So saying he fixed his red-colored eyes on the wood, and the whole pile was instantly in flames.

"You are a clever and powerful man," said Matthias. "Would you like to join our party?"

"All right, if there's no evil in it."

So the four new friends traveled along together. Matthias was quite thrilled to have met with such talented people, and he paid for their expenses as well as his own. Nor did he complain that Broad ate as much as the other three combined.

After some days they reached the princess's palace. Matthias had told them the object of his quest. "If you help me, I promise each of you a reward." They gave their word to work with him at the task, and the prince bought each of them a new suit of clothes so that they would all be quite presentable when they met the father of the princess.

"I have come with my attendants to watch three nights in the lady's bedroom." He was careful not to reveal his name or that he was a prince.

"The rules do not say that four men may stay, only one," said the king.

"It's okay, Father," said a soft voice from behind him. "I'm sure that four cannot succeed, either." When Matthias saw the princess, he fell deeply and unexpectedly in love. He shook his head, angry at himself. He had come for the challenge, and must not let his thoughts get strayed by beauty!

"Very well," said the king gravely, "but think hard on what you're about to do. If the princess should escape, the same punishment will be met by you all—each of you will lose your head."

"I doubt very much if she will escape us," said Tall, and the others agreed.

"Well, don't say I didn't warn you," smiled the king, impressed with their bravery. "You may begin now, if you like."

As they walked to the princess's apartments, Matthias caught the maiden looking at him. She could not hide that she was as pleased with him as he was of her. Still, he knew she would make it difficult for him to win her.

The king left them all in her apartments, and Broad lay down across the threshold; Tall and the Man with Eyes of

Flame sat on either side of the window, while Matthias talked with the princess, watching every move like a hawk.

Suddenly she stopped speaking, and after a moment said, "I feel as if a shower of poppies were falling on my eyelids." She yawned, stretched, and lay down on the bed, pretending to sleep.

Matthias did not say a word. Seeing her asleep he sat down at a nearby table, leaned his elbows on it, and rested his chin in the hollow of his hands. Gradually he felt drowsy and his eyes closed, as did those of his companions.

This was the moment the princess was waiting for! Quickly she transformed herself into a dove, and flew toward the window. If she had not accidently brushed Tall's hair with her wing, she would certainly have been able to escape; and if Tall had not awakened, he never would have been able to nudge Flame awake so that he could send a beam of fire in her direction. Her wings burned off, and she had to perch in a tree. Tall stretched in her direction and reached her rather easily, and placed her in Matthias' hands, where she was transformed back into a human. The prince hardly even woke up from his sleep.

The next morning and the morning after that, the king was astonished to find his daughter silently fuming by the prince's side. At the approach of the third night he pulled his daughter aside and spoke urgently to her, "I beg you, practice all the magic you can to escape. We do not know who these men are or of what rank they come from. That man could be a charcoal-burner's son or a peasant farmer for all we know!"

Before entering the woman's chamber that night, Matthias took his friends aside and said, "There is but one more stroke of luck left us, dear comrades, and then we will have succeeded! If we fail, do not forget that our four heads will roll off the scaffold. I would not blame you if you chose to back out now."

"Don't worry," Flame patted him on the shoulder. "We shall be able to keep good watch tonight."

When they came into the princess' room, they took their positions, and Matthias sat down facing the lady. "I would much prefer to enjoy your company without having to worry when you'll 'take flight' again."

"We'll see. Perhaps you'll get your wish," said the princess. "Then again, maybe you won't."

"I'll keep watch over you now, but when you're my wife I'll be able to rest."

At midnight, when sleep was beginning to overtake the watchers, the princess stretched herself on the bed, and shut her eyes as if she were asleep.

"You've tried that twice before, dear princess," said Matthias. "Don't think for a minute I believe you're really asleep." He placed his elbows on the table, his chin in the palms of his hands, and gazed at her admiringly. But as sleep closes even the eyes of an eagle, so it shut those of the prince and his companions.

The princess sat up and whispered to the sleeping prince, "I guess you were right, I wasn't really asleep." This time she changed herself into a little fly and flew out the window. Once outside, she turned herself into a fish and, falling into the palace well, plunged and hid herself in the depths of the water. The princess would certainly have made her escape if, as a fly, she had not touched the tip of the nose of the Man with Eyes of Flame. He let out a great sneeze, opened his eyes, and was just able to see her change into a fish. There was only one place she could be, the well. He let out the alarm, and the four men ran into the courtyard. The well was very deep, but it did not matter. Tall soon stretched himself out and searched in all of the corners, but he was not able to find the little fish. "I think she may have finally outsmarted us, Gentlemen."

"This is the chance I've been waiting for," said Broad. "Move aside." He stuffed his body in the well, and expanded to such a size that he squeezed all of the water out. Still, nothing was seen of the little fish.

"Let me try my luck against the clever little magician," said the Man with Eyes of Flame. When Broad stepped out of the well, the water all fell back in place. Flame fixed his gaze on the water, and it began to boil from the heat. It boiled and boiled until it bubbled over the rim, and a little fish tossed itself on the grass half-cooked. As it lay there panting, it again took the form of a princess.

Matthias ran over and kissed her tenderly. "You have conquered me, Husband," she said. "You have succeeded in preventing my escape. From now on I am yours, by right of conquest and by my own free will."

"I came here for the challenge, Princess, and I would have freely let you go. But you have conquered my heart, and I know I cannot turn my back and leave."

"Can you believe this fluff?" Broad nudged Tall in the ribs. "Okay you two, let's get back to the palace."

The young man's courtesy, bravery, strength, and gentleness pleased the princess, but her father was not happy. "I will not let my daughter go off with a man with no name."

Matthias ignored him, and the princess left with the four men. The king was furious, and he sent his guards out to bring the comrades back on pain of death. The five travelers had already gone a great way when they heard footsteps gaining on them. It was a large army of men on horseback, advancing at full gallop.

"Those are my father's guards," said the princess. "They won't be easy to escape." She took off her veil and threw it behind her saying, "I command as many trees to spring up as there are threads in this veil."

In the blink of an eye a high, thick forest rose up between them. By the time the soldiers had cleared a pathway through the dense mass, Matthias and his friends had gained quite a bit of ground.

Soon, the soldiers were gaining on them again and the princess let a tear fall from her eye. "Become a river!" she shouted. A wide river flowed between them and the soldiers, and before the army was able to cross it, Matthias and his party were far in the lead.

After another short while, the soldiers were upon them, and the princess shouted, "Darkness, cover them!" Tall drew himself up, he stretched and stretched and stretched until he reached the clouds, and with his hat he half-covered the face of the sun. On the soldiers' side it was as black as night, while for Matthias and his party the sun continued to shine.

They were nearly in sight of Matthias' home when the guards found their way out of the darkness. "Now it is my turn," said Broad. "Go on. I will lie in wait for them."

He quietly waited their arrival, standing perfectly still, with his great mouth open from ear to ear. The army, who by now were determined to let nothing stand in their way, charged toward the town at full gallop. Mistaking Broad's open mouth for one of the city gates, they all dashed through and disappeared.

Broad closed his mouth, swallowed, and smiled; then he hurried to catch up with his comrades at the palace of Matthias' father.

"Ah, here you are, Broad," Matthias said. "What did you do with the army?"

"The army is here, quite safe," he answered, patting his enormous stomach. "Although I'm afraid they'll give me indigestion."

"Come on now," laughed the princess. "Let them out of their prison."

Broad stood in the middle of the palace square, put his hands on his sides, and began to cough. It was really a sight to see! He coughed up horses and horsemen, one over the other, each trying to scramble away as quickly as possible. He had a bit of trouble with the last one, who somehow got stuck in one of Broad's nostrils. The only way to release him was by a good sneeze, and that's exactly what he did. The soldiers were sent packing back to their own kingdom.

A few days later there was a splendid feast and wedding for the prince and princess. The king, her father, was also there. Tall had been sent to fetch him. The king was delighted to know that his daughter had made such a good match, and Matthias generously rewarded his brave traveling companions, who remained with him to the end of their days.

The Dwarf with the Long Beard

In a far distant kingdom there lived a king, and he had only one daughter; a daughter who was so very beautiful that no one in the whole realm could compare with her. Her name was Princess Pietnotka, and the tales of her beauty spread from sea to sea. There were many kings and princes who sought her hand, but she had already given her heart to Prince Dobrotek. They obtained her father's blessings and consent to their marriage, and then, attended by all of the princess's handmaidens and guards, they set off for the church.

Most of the unsuccessful suitors sadly returned to their own kingdoms after the princess had made her choice. One of them, however, stayed. He was a dwarf who was only seven inches tall, with an enormous hump on his back and a beard that was seven feet long. He was a prince and a powerful magician. He was furious at being rejected, and swore to get revenge. "How dare she not choose me. I am every bit as good as Dobrotek, if not better!" He changed himself into a whirlwind and lay in wait for the princess.

When the wedding procession was mounting the steps to the church, the air around them was suddenly filled with a blinding cloud of dust, and Pietnotka was snatched away and borne up high as the highest clouds, and then disappeared. Although the people did not know it, the dwarf had taken her to his own underground palace. Then he himself vanished, leaving the princess in a lifeless condition.

After some time she opened her eyes, and found herself in a wonderful bedroom. "Some king must have run away with me!" she thought. "I hope Dobrotek will find me soon!" She got out of bed and began to explore her surroundings when all of a sudden unseen hands set the table with gold and silver dishes, and carried in cakes and breads of every description. They looked so delicious that despite her sorrow she could not resist sampling them, and she continued to eat until she was quite stuffed. She returned to the bed and lay down to rest, but was unable to sleep. It was only then that she thought to try the door.

As she sat up, the door suddenly opened by itself, and in came four servants, fully armed, and bearing a golden throne on their shoulders, upon which sat the evil little Dwarf with the Long Beard. He approached the princess and tried to kiss her, but she slapped him so hard that he went tumbling across the room; a thousand stars swam before his eyes and a thousand bells rang in his ears. He let out such a roar of rage that the castle walls shook. "Why, you hussy, you! You who are so proud, I will . . . I will . . ." He left the threat unfinished and his face softened. His love for the princess was so great that he would not show her his anger. "I will let you have your peace," he finished, and turned away to leave her. But the poor little dwarf became entangled in his long beard, and he fell flat on his face, dropping the cap he held in his hand. Now this cap had the power to make its wearer invisible. The servants hurried to rush their master out of the room, and the hat was forgotten.

When the princess found herself alone she jumped out of bed and tried on the cap. "I wonder if this will suit me?" she said to herself as she turned toward the mirror. Imagine her surprise when she looked and saw—nothing at all! She took off the cap and her image sprang into view. "What a marvel!" Just as she put it on her head again, the door to her room burst violently open, and the dwarf entered with his beard tied up. He looked all around and saw neither princess nor cap.

"I must then assume that you are wearing my cap, my dear," the dwarf growled, and he began to search the room; he felt under all the furniture, behind the curtains, even underneath the carpets! But he was searching in vain, for the princess had already crept past him, still invisible, and had left the palace entirely. She was roaming the garden, which was the largest and most beautiful one she had ever seen. There she ate the delicious fruit and drank the clear fountain water. She could have lived there quite contentedly, if only her dear prince were with her.

The dwarf began to search the garden, and the princess toyed with his anger. She would throw fruit pits in his face, or else she would take off the cap and show herself for an instant. Then she would put it on again and laugh merrily at his rage!

One day, while playing this game, the magic cap caught in the brambles of a gooseberry bush. The princess was unable to free it in time, and the dwarf was able to seize the maiden in one hand and the cap in the other. "I've had just about enough of this, Princess," he snarled. "Just wait till I get you back to the palace! There I'll teach you a lesson you won't soon forget!" He was about to carry her off when they heard the sound of a war trumpet.

The dwarf shook with rage and muttered a thousand curses. He put a sleeping spell on the princess, set the invisible cap on her head, seized his double-bladed sword, and rose up high in the air, as high as the clouds. From there he planned to dive and deliver such a strike on the intruder that he would kill him instantly. Did his plan succeed? Have patience and listen.

When the whirlwind had upset the wedding procession and stolen away the princess, there arose a great tumult among those at court. The king, the attendants, and Prince Dobrotek searched high and low for the missing girl, calling out her name and asking everyone they met if they had seen the princess. The king, in his sorrow, declared, "Dobrotek, I blame you for not protecting Pietnotka. If you do not find my daughter and bring her back, I will have my army destroy your kingdom and have you killed." Then he turned to the other princes and nobles who helped in the search and said, "Whoever brings Pietnotka to me safe and well will have her for his wife and receive half my kingdom."

Prince Dobrotek was overwhelmed with grief and shock. What was supposed to be the happiest day of his life had become a nightmare. For three days he traveled without eating, sleeping or drinking. It was his horse who finally made the decision to stop, and as he grazed in a field, Dobrotek took a short nap. Suddenly he heard horrible cries, as if someone were screaming in pain, and he looked up to see an enormous owl tearing a hare with its claws. "I am too sad myself to see anything else suffer today," he said, and grabbed hold of the first hard thing that came to his hand. He thought it was a stone, but it was really a skull, and aiming it at the owl, he killed the bird with the first blow. The rescued hare hopped up to the man and gratefully licked his hands. "Thank you, kind prince," said the hare. "I have three young ones at home who would have perished if you had not saved me." Then it scurried to its burrow as fast as it could.

"You have my thanks, too," said a voice. Dobrotek looked around and realized that what he had mistaken for a rock was a human skull. The voice continued, "I belonged to an unhappy man who took his own life rather than face his problems, and for this crime of suicide I have been condemned to lie in the mud until I was able to save the life of one of God's creatures. Before now I thought that it would be impossible. How was I, a skull, to accomplish that? For seven hundred and seventy years I miserably waited, and now you have been the means of my salvation. In return for this kindness, I will teach you how to call to your aid a most wondrous horse—a magical horse. During my lifetime he belonged to me."

"What does this horse do?" asked the prince.

"Oh, he will be able to help you in a thousand ways, and when you are in need of him you only have to walk out on the moorland without looking behind you, and say:

> *'Dappled Horse with Mane of Gold*
> *Horse of Wonder! Come to me.*
> *Walk not the earth, for I am told*
> *you fly like birds o'er land and sea.'"*

"Finish your work of mercy by burying me here, so that I may be at rest until Judgment Day."

The prince dug a hole at the foot of a tree, and there he buried the now-silent skull, and said prayers for the soul of the man. Just as he finished, he saw a tiny blue flame leap from the skull and fly toward heaven. It was the soul of the dead man on its way home.

Prince Dobrotek made the sign of the cross and resumed his journey. When he had gone some way along the moorland he stopped, and without looking back tried out the magic words:

> *"Dappled Horse with Mane of Gold*
> *Horse of Wonder! Come to me.*
> *Walk not the earth, for I am told*
> *you fly like birds o'er land and sea."*

There were flashes of lightning and peals of thunder, and then the horse appeared. Did I say a horse? More like a miracle, he was. He was as light as air, with a dappled coat and a shining gold mane. Flames came from his nostrils and sparks from his eyes. Steam poured from his mouth and smoke came from his ears. He was all magic and fire and wonder. Bowing low before the prince, he asked in a human voice, "What are your orders, Prince Dobrotek?"

"I am in a lot of trouble," answered the prince. "I would be most grateful if you could help me." Then he told all that had happened to him, and how the king threatened him with death if he did not find the princess. "Although I know I should die of sorrow anyway if I cannot find her," he sighed.

"Well," the horse neighed, "enter in at my left ear, and come out at my right."

The prince obeyed, despite the fact that it was an odd request, and he came out at the right ear clad in a suit of splendid armor. His gilded cuirass, his steel helmet inlaid with gold, and his sword and club made him into a magnificent-looking warrior. He felt empowered with superhuman strength, bravery and wisdom. When he stomped his foot the earth shook. When he shouted the trees trembled and dropped their leaves.

"What must we do now?" he asked. "Where are we to go? I hope you have a better idea of where the princess is than I do."

The horse replied, "Your bride, Princess Pietnotka, has been carried away by the jealous Dwarf with the Long Beard. This powerful magician has caused trouble for many, and must be defeated. But he lives far, far away from here, farther than you can walk in a lifetime. Nothing can touch or wound him except the sharp, biting sword that belongs to his own brother, a monstrous creature with the head and the eyes of a Basilisk."

"I suppose we must defeat him first," said Dobrotek, and leaped on the back of the Dappled Horse. They set off immediately, leaping over mountains, flying through forests, crossing rivers. So light was the steed's step that he left no mark of his passage, and the prince felt as if he were riding on air. At

last they reached a vast stretch of plain, littered with human bones. They stopped in front of a huge moving mountain, and the horse said:

"My prince, this mountain is the head of the Monster with Basilisk Eyes, and the bones that are strewn over the ground are the bones of his victims. Beware of the eyes that deal death. Never before has one escaped him, but there is always a chance for you to be the first."

"Thank you for your encouraging words," the prince said sarcastically.

The horse ignored him. "The midday heat has made the giant sleep," it said, "and the sword with the never-failing blade lies before him. Bend down and lie along my neck until we are near enough, then seize the sword. Afterward you have nothing more to fear; without his sword the monster will be unable to harm you, and will be completely at your mercy."

The horse crept up to the huge creature, and the prince quickly snatched up the sword. He sat straight in the saddle, and gave a "Hurrah!" loud enough to wake the dead. The giant lifted his head, yawned, and turned his blood-thirsty eyes upon the intruders. "I smell Christian blood," he said in a gravelly voice, "and I am particularly fond of the taste of Christian meat." Then his poisonous eyes fell on the sword and he became quiet. "Knight, is it weariness of life that brings you here?"

"Quit your boasting," replied the prince. "You are in my power and you know it. Your glance has already lost its potency, or I would be dead in my tracks. You will soon die by your own sword. But first, tell me more about yourself."

"It is true that I am in your hands, but please grant me your pity. I deserve it. I am a knight from the race of giants, and if it were not for the wickedness of my brother, I should have lived in peace. He is a horrible, nasty dwarf, and was jealous of my fine figure. You must know that his strength, which is unbelievable, lies in his beard, and it can only be cut off by the sword in your hand. One day he came to me and said, 'Dear brother, I beg you to help me to discover a sword that has been hidden in the earth by a magician. He is an enemy to you and I, and he alone can destroy us both.' What a fool I was! I believed him, and by means of a large oak tree, I raked up the mountain and found the sword. We argued then as to which of us should have it, and at last my brother suggested that we decide by lot. 'Let us each put an ear to the ground, and the sword shall belong to him who first hears the bells of that distant church,' he said. I placed my ear to the ground, and my brother struck off my head! My body became a mountain, now covered with forests. As for my head, it is full of life and strength, as you see now, and has remained here ever since to frighten away all who attempt to steal the sword. Now, Prince, I beg you to use the sword to cut off my brother's beard. Kill him, and return here to put an end to me. I will die happy if I know I am avenged."

"That you shall be, and soon. I promise you," said the prince, deeply moved.

The prince ordered the Dappled Horse with Golden Mane to take him to the Dwarf with the Long Beard. They reached the garden gate at the very moment when the dwarf had caught sight of Princess Piernotka and was running after her. He blew the war trumpet in challenge, and the dwarf was forced to meet the intruder—but not before hiding the princess with the invisible cap.

As he waited for the dwarf to answer his challenge, the prince heard a great noise in the clouds above him, and looked up to see the dwarf diving toward him. "Treacherous little toad!" he shouted and swerved to miss the swing of the ax. The dwarf fell so heavily to the ground that his body was half-buried in the earth. The prince grabbed him by the beard, and with one stroke of the sword gave the dwarf a close shave.

He tied the dwarf to his saddle, put the beard in his helmet, and entered the palace. When the servants saw that he had really cut the beard off their cruel master, they opened all of the doors to give him entrance. The dwarf refused to tell him where he had hidden the girl, and without wasting any time, the prince began to search for the princess. For a long time he searched, quite unsuccessfully, and was near the end of his rope when he tripped over her quite accidentally, knocking off the invisible cap. "Pietnotka!" he cried, beholding his lovely bride sound asleep. But no matter how loudly he shouted, he was unable to wake her. The dwarf would not tell him how to break the spell, so the prince took his love in his arms, mounted the steed, and shoved the dwarf in his pocket. "Take me back to the giant," he ordered his horse.

The Monster with the Basilisk Eyes swallowed the dwarf in one mouthful, and the prince cut the monster's head up into a million pieces, which he scattered over the plain. The creature was at last in peace.

Then the prince continued his journey. Coming to the moorland, the Dappled Horse suddenly stopped. "My prince," he said, "we must part our ways for the time being. You are not far from home, and your own horse awaits you; but before you go, enter in my right ear and come out my left."

The prince did so, and came out without his armor, and clad as when Pietnotka had disappeared. The Dappled Horse with the Mane of Gold vanished, and Dobrotek whistled to his own horse, who ran up, quite eager to see his master again. They immediately set off for the king's palace.

Night came on quicker then expected, and they needed a place to settle. The prince laid the sleeping girl on the grass, and fell asleep at her side. By chance a knight, one of the princess's old suitors, passed that way. Seeing Dobrotek asleep, he drew his sword and stabbed him, then lifted the princess on his horse and reached the king's palace. "Here is your daughter," he smugly said to the king. "I now claim her as my wife, for it is I who have restored her to you."

"Where was she?" asked the king.

"She was . . . um, she, she was captured by a terrible and wicked sorcerer. That's right. For three days and three nights we

were locked in mortal combat, but I conquered him, and I have brought you the princess safely back."

"But why won't she awaken? What has been done to her?" asked the king dubiously.

"Well, you see, it's like this . . . I, I don't know. This is how I found her."

Meanwhile, the girl's true love lay seriously wounded, his life's blood pouring out of him. He barely had enough strength to utter these words:

"Come, Magic Horse with Mane of Gold
Come, Dappled Horse, oh come to me.
Fly like the birds as you did of old,
As flashes of lightning o'er land and sea."

A bright cloud formed before him, and out stepped his old friend. He did not need to be told what happened, but dashed off immediately to the Mountain of Eternal Life. There he drew three kinds of water: the Water that Gives Life, the Water that Cures, and the Water that Strengthens. Returning to the prince, he sprinkled him first with the Life-Giving Water, and instantly the body, which was cold, was warm again and the blood began to circulate. The Water that Cures closed the wounds, and the Strength-Giving water had such an effect upon him that he jumped to his feet and shouted, "I feel one hundred percent better! Let's go!"

"You were sleeping the eternal sleep," replied the horse. "One of your rivals stabbed you and you died. He carried off Princess Pietnotka, whom he pretends to have rescued. Don't worry, however, she still sleeps, and no one can rouse her but you."

"How am I to do that?" asked the prince.

"You must touch her with the dwarf's beard," said the horse simply.

"And why didn't you tell me this before?"

"You didn't ask," neighed the horse, and disappeared in a whirlwind of dust.

The prince made it back to the king's palace in time to see it surrounded by an enemy army. The prince put on his invisible cap, and began to strike right and left with the sharp sword. With such fury and strength did he attack the enemy that they fell dead on all sides, like chopped trees. When he had destroyed the whole army he went, still invisible, into the palace where he heard the king say, "Why has the army so suddenly disappeared? Who is the brave warrior who saved us?"

Everyone was silent, unable to answer, and Dobrotek took off his magic cap. "It is I, my king and father, who destroyed the enemy. It is I who saved the princess, my rightful bride. On our way back I was killed by my rival, who has told you he rescued the princess. But he has deceived you all. Take me to the princess. I know how to awaken her."

The imposter left the kingdom as quickly as possible, lucky to have escaped with his life. Dobrotek approached the sleeping maiden and touched her cheek with the dwarf's beard. She opened her eyes and smiled. "What a strange dream I've had," she said.

The king kissed her fondly, and that same evening she was married to the prince. The king himself led her to the altar, and gave his son-in-law half the kingdom. Afterward, he pulled the prince aside and said, "Seldom it is that a king will admit his wrong, but I owe you an apology. There is none more faithful to my daughter than you."

The Girl with the Hair of Gold

There was once a king who was so wise and clever that he understood the language of all birds and beasts. He was not born with the talent, however; he had to earn that power. You shall hear how it all came to be.

One day an old and bent woman came to the king's palace. "I wish to speak to his majesty at once," she demanded. "I have something of great importance to tell him."

"The king is a very busy man," said the guard. "I will take your message to him."

"No, I must speak with him myself!" The woman was so insistent that the guard finally admitted her to the king's presence. She presented him with a strange-looking fish.

"What is this, Woman?" the king tried to hide a smile. "I have already eaten my supper."

"It doesn't matter," replied the woman, ignoring the king's look of amusement. "Have it cooked for yourself, and when you have eaten it you will understand all that is said by the birds of the air, the animals that walk on land, and the fish that live under the waters."

The king greatly desired to know things that no one else knew, so he rewarded the woman with a purse of gold. He ordered a servant to cook the fish. "But take care," the monarch cautioned, "that you do not taste it yourself. If you do you will be killed."

The servant, whose name was George, was astonished to receive such a threat. "Now why is my master so anxious that no one else eat this fish? What is so special about it?" he thought. It didn't even look like any kind of fish he knew. "Never in all my life have I seen such an odd-looking creature," he thought. "It seems more like a reptile than a fish." The servant decided there was no harm in tasting a little piece of the fish. After all, it was his right as a cook.

When the fish was fried he tasted a small piece, and while he was sampling the sauce he heard a buzzing voice speaking close to his ear.

"Let us take a crumb, let us taste a little," the voice said. He looked all around to see where the words came from, but there were only a few flies buzzing about in the kitchen. Then the servant heard a rough, croaking voice from out in the yard, "Where are we going to settle? Where?"

"How about in the miller's barley field?" another rough and hoarse voice answered.

When George looked out the window all he saw was a gander flying at the head of a flock of geese. Were they the source of the voices?

"What luck!" he thought. "Now I know why my master set so much stock in this fish, and why he wished it all to himself. It's magic!" George knew beyond a shadow of a doubt that by tasting the fish he had learned the language of the animals, so after sampling a little more he served the king with the remainder, carefully arranging it so that it looked as if nothing had been eaten.

When the king finished eating he ordered George to saddle two horses and accompany him for a ride. They were soon off, the king in front, the servant behind.

While crossing a field, George's horse began to prance about, neighing out these words, "I say, Brother, I feel so light and high-spirited today that in one single bound I could leap over to those mountains."

"I could do the same," the king's horse answered grumpily, "but I carry this feeble old geezer on my back; he would fall like a log and break his skull open."

"What do you care?" said the other horse. "So much the better if he did break his head! Then instead of being ridden by a decrepit old man you would probably be mounted by a handsome young one."

The servant smothered a laugh when he heard this conversation. He did not want the king to hear him. Even so, the king turned around in time to see a smirk on his servant's face. "What are you laughing at, Man?" he asked, his eyes narrow and searching.

"Oh, nothing, Sire. Nothing at all. Just a foolish thought that went through my head."

The king said nothing, and asked no more questions, but he was suspicious and didn't trust the servant or the horses. "Let's go back to the palace. I'm growing tired."

When they arrived he said to George, "Get me some wine, but mind you only pour enough to fill the glass, for if you put in one drop too much, so that it overflows, I shall certainly order my executioner to cut off your head at the shoulders. You may be sure I'll do as I say."

"Now what could have put the king in such a snit?" the servant thought. As he turned to get the wine two birds flew near the window, one chasing after the other, which carried three golden hairs in its beak.

"Give them to me," said the one. "You know that they are mine. I spotted them first!"

"Too bad!" chirped the other. "I picked these up myself."

"It doesn't matter! I'm the one who saw them fall while the Maid with Locks of Gold was combing her hair. You could be honest and at least share them with me! Give me one and keep the other two for yourself!"

"No, not a single one! They're all mine! Mine! Mine! Mine!"

The birds began to fight over the hair, and in their struggle one of the strands fell so that it struck the ground with a metallic tinkle. George was so completely taken off his guard that the wine he was pouring overflowed the glass.

The king was furious, and feeling convinced that his servant had disobeyed him and had tasted the fish as well, said, "You thief! You scoundrel! You deserve death for disobeying me! Nevertheless, I will not hang you if you bring me the Maid with the Golden Locks. I intend to make her my wife."

The lad was found out! What was to be done now? Poor

fellow, he was willing to do anything to save his own hide, of course, even run the risk of losing it on a long journey. He was left with no choice other than to search for the Maid with the Golden Locks. "Okay," he said, "I'll go." But where was he to begin?

When the servant had saddled and mounted his horse he allowed it its own head, and it carried him to the edge of a dark forest. There some shepherds had left a bush burning, and the sparks of the fire from the bush threatened the lives of a large number of ants which had built their hill close by. The poor little things were scurrying back and forth, rushing in all directions to rescue their tiny eggs. George jumped down from his horse, cut down the bush and put out the fire.

"Thank you, thank you!" the ants said. George had to bend down so that he could hear their tiny voices. "Whenever you are in trouble, Sir, you only need call us. We'll help! We'll help!"

The young fellow nodded and continued on his way until he was deep, deep into the forest. There he came upon a very tall fir tree. At the top of the tree sat a raven's nest, while at the foot lay two young ones who were calling out to their parents. "Mother, Father!" they chirped. "Where have you gone? You have flown away and we need food! Our wings don't have any feathers yet. How can we fly? How will we eat?"

Without stopping to think, George dismounted, and with his sword killed the horse to provide food for the little birds. They thanked him and said, "If ever you should be in trouble, call on us and we will be there at once to help you. Well, at least as soon as our feathers grow."

George now had to travel on foot, and he walked for a long time, going far, and farther than far, into the forest. When he finally reached the other side, he saw stretching before him a wide sea. On the shore two men were arguing over the possession of a fish with golden scales.

"The net belongs to me," said one of them, "so the fish is mine."

"You would have lost both the fish and the net if I had not come along just in time with my boat."

"Then you shall have the next haul that I make," said the owner of the net.

"Oh, sure. Suppose you catch nothing? No. Give me this one and keep the next catch for yourself."

"I'll put an end to the quarrel," interrupted George. "Sell me the fish. I will pay you well, and you can split the money between you."

He handed over all the money the king had given him for the journey, without keeping a single coin for himself. The fishermen danced all of the way home, hardly believing their luck; but George didn't eat the fish, he put it back in the water.

"Thank you," said the fish, splashing about in the water. "I thought I was a goner for sure. Whenever you need my help you only have to call me, I won't fail you!"

"I do have one question you may be able to help with," said George. "I am looking for a wife for my old master. She is known as the Maid with the Golden Locks. Only I have no idea of how to find her."

"If that's all you need, I can easily give you the information. She is Princess Zlato Vlaska, daughter of the king whose crystal palace is built on that island over there. Every morning when she combs her hair, the golden light is reflected on sea and sky. I'll take you to the island, if you want. But you should be aware of one thing: when you're in the palace don't make a mistake in choosing your princess—there are twelve of them, but only Zlato Vlaska has hair of gold."

George sat on the back of the fish and it took him to the island. When he got there he wasted no time in demanding from the king the hand of his daughter, the Princess Zlato Vlaska, for his master.

"With pleasure I'll wed my daughter to your king," said his majesty, "but I do have one condition. You must perform certain tasks, tasks that I will set for you. There will be three, and they must be completed in three days."

"That's fine," said George. "When can I start?"

"Ho!" the king laughed. "For the present you should rest and refresh yourself."

The next morning the king said, "My daughter, the Maid with the Golden Hair, had a string of beautiful pearls. The thread broke and the pearls were scattered far and wide in the meadow. I want you to go and pick up every one—each and every single one—and bring them to me."

George searched the field for the pearls. It was a great meadow which stretched all the way to the horizon. He bent down on his hands and knees and hunted between the grass and weeds from morning until noon, but not a single pearl could he find. Where were they?

"If only I had my little friends, the ants," he said, "they would surely be able to help me."

"No sooner said than done," answered a little voice by his elbow. He looked around and saw thousands of little ants surrounding him. "What is wrong?" they asked. "How can we help?"

"I have to find a string of pearls that were scattered around the field, only I can't see a single one. Do you think you can spot them?"

"Wait a while, and we will help you," they said.

It was not long before the ants brought him a heap of pearls, and all he had left to do was to restring them. Just as he was about to make a knot at the end, he saw another ant hobbling up to him. One of her feet had been burned in the fire, and she could only move slowly. "Wait a moment, George!" she said. "Don't tie the knot yet, not until you get the last pearl!"

George took the pearls back to the palace, and the king counted them. "You surprise me, Sir," he said. "But I have a second task for you. My daughter, the Princess Zlato Vlaska, dropped her ring into the sea while swimming. You must find the jewel and return it to me by sunset."

The young servant walked up and down the beach. The water was crystalline clear, but he could not see beyond a certain distance, nor did he know how to swim. "Ah, my golden fish, why are you not here now? You would surely be able to help me find the ring."

"Here I am," answered a bubbly voice from the sea. "What can I do for you?"

"I have to find the princess's golden ring, but I don't know how to swim, so there's little use looking."

"You don't say? Just this morning I met a pike wearing a gold ring on his fin. Will you wait a moment for me?" In a short time he resurfaced with the pike and his ring. The pike willingly gave up the jewel. "Who am I to stand in the way of love?" he said.

The king thanked George for the return of the ring. "I have only one more task for you. If you really want to win the hand of my daughter for your king, you must bring me two things that I want more than anything: the Water of Death and the Water of Life."

George had no idea how he was to find these waters, and how he was to find them in one day! He went first in one direction, and then in the other, until he reached the forest.

"If my raven friends were here, I'm sure they'd be able to help me."

Suddenly he heard a rushing noise, and then came the ravens calling "Krak! Krak! Krak! Here we are, ready and willing to do what we can! What do you need?"

"Your feathers have grown!" the servant called happily. "I need to collect a vial of the Water of Life and another of the Water of Death. I don't know where to find these, do you?"

"Krak! Certainly we do. Wait here a moment."

Off they flew, and it was not long before they returned, each with a small vial in his beak. One vial contained the Water of Life and the other held the Water of Death.

George was astonished with their success, and he hurried back to the palace. When he was near the edge of the forest, he saw a spider's web hanging between two fir trees. At the very center the spider was devouring a fly he had just killed. George decided to test the waters, and he sprinkled a few drops of the Water of Death on the spider. Immediately it stiffened and fell to the ground like a stone. Then he sprinkled a few drops of the Water of Life on the fly, and she began to stir, and gradually freed herself from the spider's webbing. Then she spread her wings and flew around the servant's head. "You have guaranteed your own happiness by restoring mine. Without my help you would never have recognized the Princess with the Golden Hair. Tomorrow you must select her from among the twelve sisters, and I will be there to point out the right one."

The next morning George was led to a large room and asked to choose Zlato from among the twelve daughters who sat at the table. Each wore a linen headdress that completely hid her hair, and in such a way the servant could not guess who had what color hair.

"Well," said the king, "here are my daughters. Lovely girls, all, but only one of them has golden hair. If you find her she may go with you, but if you are wrong you will return to your king empty-handed."

George blushed in embarrassment, not knowing how to choose.

"BZZZZZ! BZZZZZ!" said a voice in his ear. "I told you I'd be here. Now walk around each of these girls, and I will tell you which is the Princess Zlato Vlaska."

Reassured, George walked around the table. At each chair he stopped and said, "This is not the one with the hair of gold."

Suddenly the fly buzzed excitedly, "This is the one! Here is Princess Zlato Vlaska herself! Claim her quickly! Quickly!"

"She is the one," said George, placing his hand on the girl's shoulder. "I take her in the name of my king."

"You have guessed right," said the king sadly. "I will keep my word."

The princess rose from her seat, and let the headdress fall back. Cascades of golden hair tumbled down like a waterfall, catching the rays of the morning light. The young man's eyes were dazzled, and he fell in love with her on sight.

The king sent many gifts with his daughter, and she left the home of her father to follow this strange young man into an unknown future.

When they arrived, the old king was delighted with the sight of Zlato Vlaska. "She is even more beautiful than I thought," he said. Preparations were made for a wedding feast, and all the nobles of the land were invited.

The king drew George aside. "I know that you robbed me of the secret of animal language. For this reason I planned on having your head cut off and your body thrown to the wolves. But since you have served me so faithfully and so well, I will not do that. You will still be executed, do not doubt that, but you will be buried with all the honors worthy of a high-ranking noble."

"What . . ." the astonished servant found he could not speak.

The cruel sentence was carried out, and the Princess with the Golden Hair begged the king to make her a present of George's body. The ruler was so in love with the young maiden that he could not refuse her anything.

Zlato Vlaska had with her the vial of the Water of Life. She poured this water over George's poor, broken body, and he instantly returned to life, as hale and hearty as he was before. "What a sleep I've had!" he said and stretched.

"Yes, you did sleep soundly. No one has ever awakened from so sound a sleep," the princess smiled.

When the king saw George returned to life, looking younger, stronger, more handsome and more vigorous than ever, he too wanted to be made young again. He therefore ordered his servants to cut off his head and sprinkle it with the life-giving water. They did cut it off, but he did not come to life again, although they poured all that was left of the water over his body. Perhaps they made some mistake in using the water, or perhaps the princess instead gave them the Water of Death. In any case, there was no water left, no one knew where to get any, and no one could understand the language of the animals.

To make a long story shorter, George was declared the new king—everyone was rather impressed with his resurrection—and the Princess with the Golden Hair, who loved him for his bravery and honesty, became his queen.

The Journey to the Sun and the Moon

There was once a young maiden and a young man who loved each other dearly. The youth's name was Gene, the girl was called Annette. Folks said that in her sweetness Annette resembled a dove; in her strength and bravery she was likened to an eagle.

Annette's father was a wealthy farmer, and he owned a large estate with vast fields. Gene's father, however, was only a poor mountain shepherd. Annette, of course, did not care that the young man was poor, for he was rich in love and goodness. Nor did she suspect that her father would have any objections to their marriage.

One day Gene put on his best holiday clothes, and went to ask the farmer for his daughter's hand. The farmer listened carefully to the young man's case, nodding now and then but not interrupting, and then he said, "You wish to marry my Annette, hmm? Well, it won't be easy parting with her, for she is more precious to me than all of my wealth. You must first do a brave deed, just as kings and princes must. Go then and ask the Sun why he does not warm the night as well as the day, then seek out the Moon and inquire of her why she does not shine by day as well as by night. The day you bring me these answers is the day that I will let you wed my daughter and have my farm."

Gene was not put off by these conditions; quite the contrary. He expected to face a challenge and he was not disappointed. So he placed his hat on his head and took a loving farewell of Annette before he set out in search of the Sun. He walked all day long, and he walked far, and at dusk he reached a small village. He looked for a place to spend the night, and found shelter with some kind people who also offered him supper. "Where are you traveling?" they asked him.

"I'm off to visit the Sun and the Moon. There are a few things I would like to ask them," he said.

"You don't say!" exclaimed the father of the household. "Would you then mind asking the Sun why the village pear tree, which for years had borne the finest fruit, has now stopped producing?"

"I'll do what I can," Gene promised.

He walked on and on, over mountain and moor, through meadows and thick wood, until he came to a land where there was no drinking water to be found. The inhabitants of this land, when they heard where Gene was going, begged him to ask the Sun and the Moon why their well no longer gave good water. "It was the main supply of water for us," he was told. Gene promised to do what he could, and then continued his journey.

After days and days of walking, the young lover at last reached the home of the Sun. "Oh, Sun!" Gene said. "Might I have a moment of your time?"

The Sun looked at him impatiently, "Be quick then. I was about to leave on my daily rounds, and already you delay me.

"Do tell me, why do you not warm the earth by night?"

"That's easy enough, if I did the earth would have no time to cool. It would soon burn itself to a cinder, taking all life with it."

Gene also asked about the pear tree and the well, to which the Sun replied, "I don't think I can help you there. My sister, the Moon, would know better than I."

The Sun quickly hurried off, and Gene traveled far and fast to meet with the Moon. When he finally caught up to her he asked, "Would you kindly take a moment to answer a few questions for me?"

"Be quick," she sighed. "The Earth is waiting for me."

"Tell me, dear Moon, why you do not light the world by day as well as by night, and why do you never warm it?"

"If I lit up both day and night the plants would produce neither flower nor fruit. Although I don't warm the earth, I do supply it with the dew that makes it fertile and fruitful."

She was about to hurry on her way when Gene stopped her with the other questions.

"I know the problem with the pear tree. While the king's oldest daughter remained unmarried, the tree bore fruit every year. After her wedding she had a child who died and who was buried under that tree. If the child is given a proper Christian burial, the tree will produce fruit just as before.

"As to the water, the problem is under the mouth of the well. Just where the water should flow lies an enormous toad which poisons it constantly. Kill the toad and the troubles are over."

The Moon then continued her journey, and Gene watched her go, having no more questions to ask.

He went home to claim Annette, but first stopped at the land that was short of water. The inhabitants were anxiously waiting to hear what news he brought. He told them what the Moon had said, and sure enough, right under the brim of the well they found a horrible ugly toad which poisoned the water. When they killed it, the water became pure and transparent, and sweet to the taste.

The people all brought Gene gifts, and he set off for home weighed down with riches. When he got to the town with the barren pear tree, he was warmly welcomed by the king, who at once asked him if he had remembered his promise.

"I never forget a promise once I make one," said Gene. "But it's a sad story I bring back to you."

He then told the people what the Moon had said, and when the child was given a proper burial, the tree sprouted blossoms again. Gene was weighed down by still more presents, and the king gave him a most valuable horse, "So you can return all the more quickly to your Annette."

Annette was wild with happiness when she saw her lover's safe return. Her father, however, felt quite differently. He had hoped to never see Gene again, and had only sent him on this quest because he thought he would be burned up by the Sun's heat. But the shepherd returned, not only safe and sound but also very rich—and very knowledgeable. He now knew more about the Sun and the Moon than any other person alive.

Annette's father now had nothing left to complain about, and the wedding of his daughter and Gene was celebrated with great joy and feasting. Large amounts of roasted crane were eaten, and glasses overflowed with mead. So beautiful, too, was the music that for many years afterward it was heard to echo among the mountains and valleys. Even now its sweet tones are sometimes heard. I myself once heard the music.

The King of the Mineral Kingdom

Once upon a time, and a long, long time ago it was, there lived a widow who had a very pretty daughter. The mother was a good and honest soul, and was quite happy with her station in life, but her daughter was otherwise. She, like all spoiled beauties, looked down with contempt at her many admirers. She was full of proud and ambitious thoughts, and the more lovers she attracted, the prouder she became.

One beautiful moonlit night the mother awoke, and unable to sleep, she began to pray that God bring happiness to her only child, although she often had made her mother's life miserable. The woman looked lovingly at the daughter lying next to her, and she wondered, as she saw her smile in her sleep, what happy dream had visited her. She finished her prayer, and laying her head on her pillow, soon fell asleep.

The next day she said, "Come here, Daughter, and tell me what you were dreaming last night. You looked so happy smiling in your sleep."

"Oh, yes, I remember what it was. I had a very beautiful dream! I thought a rich nobleman came to our house in a splendid carriage of brass, and gave me a ring set with stones. How it sparkled like the stars in heaven! When I entered the church with him it was full of people, and they all thought me as beautiful, divine and adorable as the Blessed Virgin herself!"

"My child, what sin! May God keep you from having such dreams!"

"Oh, pooh!" The daughter kissed her mother on the cheek, and ran away singing. That same morning a handsome young farmer drove into the village in his cart and begged them to come and share his country bread. He was a kind and respectable fellow, and the mother liked him very much. But the daughter refused his invitation, and insulted him in the bargain. "Even if you had driven in a carriage of brass, and offered me a ring set with stones shining as the stars in heaven, I would never have married you! You are nothing but a mere peasant!"

The young farmer was terribly upset and returned home a saddened man. The mother turned to her daughter and scolded, "How dare you put on such airs! You yourself come from a humble home!"

The next night the woman again woke, and taking her rosary prayed even more intensely that God would bless her child. This time the girl laughed in her sleep.

"What can the child possibly be dreaming about?" the woman said to herself. Sighing, she finished her prayers, laid her head upon the pillow, and tried in vain to sleep. In the morning as her daughter dressed, the mother said, "Well, my dear, you were dreaming again last night, and laughing like a maniac."

"Was I? I suppose it's possible. I dreamt a nobleman came for me in a silver carriage, and gave me a golden diadem. When I entered the church with him, the people admired and worshipped me more than the Blessed Virgin."

"What a terrible dream that was! What a wicked dream! Pray God not to lead you into temptation." She scolded her daughter severely, and then stomped out of the house, slamming the door behind her.

That same morning a carriage drove into the village, and some gentlemen invited the mother and daughter to share the bread of the lord of the manor. The mother curtsied low—she knew this was a great honor—but the daughter sniffed and said, "Even if you had come to fetch me in a carriage of solid silver and presented me with a gold diadem, I would never have consented to be the wife of your lord."

The men could not believe their ears, and they turned

away in disgust. The mother rebuked her daughter for having so much pride.

"Miserable, wretched, foolish girl!" she cried. "Pride is a breath from hell. It is your duty to be humble, honest and sweet-tempered—not a spoiled brat!"

The daughter only laughed at her mother.

The third night the daughter slept soundly, but the poor woman at her side could not even close her eyes. Butterflies flew about her stomach, and she feared that some misfortune was about to happen. She counted her beads, praying all the while. All at once the sleeper beside her began to sneer and laugh.

"Merciful God in Heaven!" cried the old woman. "What are these dreams that plague the brain of my beautiful daughter?"

In the morning she was almost afraid to question the girl. "What made you sneer so frightfully last night? You must have had bad dreams again, poor child."

"Don't start with me, Mother. You look all set to begin preaching again."

"No, no; but I do want to know what you were dreaming about."

"Well, if you must know, I dreamt someone drove up in a golden carriage and asked me to marry him, and he brought me a mantle of cloth of pure gold. When we came into the church, the crowd shoved and pressed forward to kneel before me."

The mother wrung her hands, and the girl quickly left the room to avoid another scolding. That same day three carriages entered the yard, one of brass, one of silver, and one of gold. The first was drawn by two white horses, the second by three, and the third by four swan-white horses. Gentlemen wearing scarlet gloves and green mantles got out of the brass and silver carriages, while from the golden carriage alighted a prince who, as the sun shown on him, looked as if he were dressed in gold. They all made their way to the widow and the prince asked for her daughter's hand.

The old woman curtsied so low her nose touched the ground, and when she spoke her voice shook, "I . . . I fear we are not worthy of so much honor." But when the daughter's eyes fell on the face of the prince, she recognized in him the lover of her dreams, and she withdrew into the house to weave an aigrette of many-colored feathers. In exchange for this aigrette which she offered her bridegroom, he placed upon her finger a ring set with stones that shone like the stars in heaven, and over her shoulders he threw a mantle of gold cloth. The young bride, beside herself with joy, retired to the house to gather her remaining things. Meanwhile the anxious mother, eaten away by the blackest forebodings, said to her son-in-law, "My daughter has agreed to share your bread, only tell me of what sort of flour it is made?"

"In our house we have bread of brass, of silver, and of gold; I am a generous man, my wife shall be free to choose."

Such a mysterious reply astonished the poor woman, and made her still more unhappy. The daughter asked no questions, and was, in fact, content to know nothing, not even what her mother suffered. She looked magnificent in her bridal dress and golden mantle, and she left her home with the prince. She did not even say good-bye to her mother or to any of her friends. Nor did she ask for her mother's blessing, although the old woman wept and prayed for her safety.

After the marriage ceremony, the pair mounted the golden carriage and set off, followed by the attendants of silver and brass. The procession moved slowly along the road without stopping until they reached the foot of a high rock. "But where is your palace?" asked the girl. "I do not see anything." Here, instead of a carriage entrance, was a large cavern which led out onto a steep slope down which the horses went lower and lower. The giant Zemo-tras (he who makes earthquakes) closed the opening with a huge stone. They made their way in darkness for some time, and the terrified bride sought to be reassured by her husband. "Where are we going? Will you answer me, please?"

"Fear nothing," he said, patting her hand. "In a little while it will be clear and beautiful. You'll see."

Grotesque dwarfs, carrying lighted torches, appeared on all sides. "Welcome, welcome King Kovlad!" they shouted as they illumined the road for him and his attendants. "You have brought us a queen!"

For the first time the girl realized the one she had married was named Kovlad, but this mattered little to her. On coming out of the gloomy passages into the open they found themselves surrounded by large forests and mountains—mountains that seemed to touch the sky. And, strange to relate, all of the trees—no matter what kind—and even the mountains were of solid lead. When they had crossed these marvelous mountains, the giant Zemo-tras closed all of the openings in the road they had passed. They then drove out upon a vast and beautiful plain, in the center of which stood a golden palace covered with precious stones. The bride was weary with looking at so many wonders (who would have thought!), and gladly sat down to the feast prepared by the dwarfs. Meats of many kinds were served, roasted and boiled, but lo! they were of metal—brass, silver and gold. Everyone ate heartily and enjoyed the food, but the young wife, with tears in her eyes, begged for a piece of bread.

"Certainly, my dear, with pleasure," answered Kovlad, but she could not eat the bread which was brought, for it was of brass. Then the king sent for a piece of silver bread. Still she could not eat it. Again he asked for a slice of bread, and the girl was brought a slice that was made of gold. She was unable to take even the tiniest bite. The servants did all they could to get something to their mistress's taste, but she found it impossible to eat anything.

"I would be most happy to satisfy you," said Kovlad, "but I don't have any other kind of food."

Then the girl realized the extent of the situation in which she had placed herself, and she began to weep bitterly and wished she had heeded her mother's advice.

"It is no use to weep and regret," said Kovlad. "You must have known the kind of bread you would have to break here. Your wish has been fulfilled."

And so it was, for nothing can recall the past. The wretched girl was obliged henceforth to live underground with her husband Kovlad, the God of Metals, in his golden palace, and all this because she had set her heart upon nothing but the possession of gold, and had never wished for anything better.

What became of her in the end? What becomes of anyone who has no food to eat?

The Three Golden Hairs

Can this be a true story? My grandmother, who told it to me, says that it is. Perhaps she is right, perhaps not, but in any case I will tell it to you.

There was once a king who was very fond of hunting, and he often sought wild beasts in the forests surrounding his kingdom. One day he followed a deer so far into the woods that he lost his way. He was all alone and night was fast approaching, so he was very glad to find himself near the small thatched cottage of a charcoal-burner.

"Can you please show me the way to the King's Road?" he asked the charcoal-burner. "I would be very grateful, and you would be richly rewarded."

The charcoal-burner wiped his forehead, leaving a smudge of soot, and looked up at the man on horseback. "Any other time I would help you," he said, "but tonight the Lord is going to send my wife another child, and I cannot leave her alone. You are welcome to spend the night here. There is a truss of sweet hay in the loft where you may sleep. Tomorrow morning I can show you the way."

The king considered this a moment, and decided that it would be fun to stay with this charming peasant and his wife. Shortly afterward, a son was born to the charcoal-burner's wife, and there was much rejoicing. When the family finally settled down for the night, the king found that he could not sleep. He tossed and he turned every which way, but he could not get comfortable.

Around midnight he heard a noise in the house. It sounded as if someone were creeping about downstairs. Looking through a crack in the flooring, the king saw the charcoal-burner and his wife sound asleep, the children in the next bed, and the newly born baby in the cradle. At the side of the cradle stood three old women dressed in white, each holding a lighted candle in her hand, and all whispering together. He knew they must be the *Soudiché*, the Fate Sisters.

"On this boy-child I bestow the gift of bravery in the face of danger," the first one said.

The second said, "I bestow the gift of happily escaping those dangers, and of living to a ripe old age."

The third sister winked and said, "I bestow upon him, for a wife, the princess born at the selfsame hour as he, the daughter of the very king who is peering down at us." All three *Soudiché* looked up at the king and grinned before they blew out their candles. Afterward there was silence.

The king was greatly troubled at these words, and wondered if he had dreamed it all. But what if he had not? He felt as if a sword blade were thrust in his chest. He lay awake all night thinking how he was to prevent the words of the Fate Sisters from coming true. His daughter must not marry a peasant!

With the first rays of the sun the baby began to cry. The charcoal-burner nudged his wife, but found her dead. He bowed his head in silent prayer before going over to the child. "Oh my poor, poor little orphan," he said sadly, "what will become of you without your mother's care?"

The king climbed down the ladder and put his hand on the peasant's shoulder. "Give your child to me," he said kindly. "I will look after him. He will be well provided for. I will also give you a yearly sum of money, so that you need never have to burn charcoal again."

The father quickly agreed to this. What poor man wouldn't? He would be able to better care for the remaining children if he did not have to work all day.

"Then it is settled," said the king. "I will send someone to fetch him."

Back at court the queen and her courtiers thought that it would be a wonderful surprise to tell the king that a daughter had been born on the night he was away, two weeks earlier than was expected. But instead of being pleased, the king frowned terribly, and he called one of his servants over. "I want you to go to a certain charcoal-burner's cottage," he growled. "I will tell you the way. Give the man this purse of gold in exchange for his newborn son. On your way back here, drown the child. See well that you complete this task, for if he should escape, you will suffer death in his place."

The servant was given the child in a basket, and on reaching the center of a narrow bridge that stretched across a wide and deep river, he threw both basket and baby into the water.

"A good journey to you, son-in-law," the king laughed when he heard the servant's story. "He is finally out of my hair and I need no longer worry."

But did the child really drown? Of course not, or else my story would be done. At that very moment the tiny baby was floating along quite contentedly, and sleeping as if his mother rocked him in her arms.

Now it just so happened that a fisherman, who was mending his nets before his cottage door, saw the basket floating down the river. "Whatever is that?" he thought, and jumped at once into his boat to pick it up. Upon seeing the contents, he ran to tell his wife the good news.

"My dear, look!" the fisherman cried. "We have always wished for a child, and here the Lord has sent us this beautiful little boy!"

The woman was delighted, and she took the infant and loved him as if it were her own child. "We shall call him Plavacek, the Floater," she said. "The name suits him well, seeing as he has come to us floating on the water."

The years passed away and the river flowed on. The tiny baby grew into a handsome young man—in all of the villages around there were none to compare with him. It happened that the king was one day riding unattended, and as the heat was very great he reined in his horse at the fisherman's door to ask for a drink of water. Plavacek brought out a mug and the king stared at him. There was something quite disturbing about the lad. He turned to the fisherman and said, "Now that's a fine-looking youth. Is he your son?"

"He is and he isn't," the fisherman smiled. "I found him when he was a tiny baby, floating down the stream in a basket. My wife and I adopted him and brought him up as our own son."

The king turned as pale as death, for he guessed that it was the same child he had ordered drowned so many years before. "Listen," he said to the fisherman, "I need a trusty messenger to take a letter back to the palace. May I send your son with it?"

"With pleasure!" the man beamed with pride. "Your Majesty may be sure of its safe delivery!"

The king wrote the following words:

My dear Queen,
The man who brings you this letter is the most dangerous of all my enemies. Have his head cut off at once, without delay and without pity. He must be executed before my return. Such is my will and pleasure.
With love, the King

The king carefully folded the letter and stamped it with his royal seal. Plavacek took the letter and set off immediately for the palace. But the forest he had to travel through was thick with trees, and he missed the path he was supposed to follow. Darkness overtook him and he nearly bumped into a withered old woman before he saw her. "Where are you going, Plavacek?" she asked. "Where are you going?"

"I am taking a letter from the king to the queen, but have lost my way. Could you point me in the direction of the royal palace?"

"Nope! Nope! It's impossible today, Child! Quite impossible! It is dark, and you would never find your way. Stay with me tonight, Plavacek, and you will not be staying with strangers. I am your godmother."

"Godmother!" Plavacek cried. "How very lucky I am to have run into you! I will gladly go back with you." She led him to a tiny little cottage that seemed suddenly to sink into the earth. While he slept the old woman exchanged his letter for another, which read thus:

My dearest Queen,

Immediately upon receipt of this letter introduce the bearer to our daughter. This is the young man I have chosen for a son-in-law, and it is my wish that they should be married before my return to the palace. Such is my pleasure.

Ever yours, the King

The letter was delivered as requested, and when the queen read it she ordered everyone to prepare themselves for a wedding. If she thought that the matter was a bit odd, she did not say anything, and kept any doubts to herself. Besides, she and her daughter greatly enjoyed Plavacek's company. Nothing disturbed the happiness of the newlywed couple.

Within a few days the king returned home. How angry he was when he heard what had happened! How dare the queen disobey him!

"What are you talking about?" the queen demanded hotly. "Did you or did you not ask me to hold a wedding before your return?! If you don't believe me, take a look at the letter yourself!"

The king peered at the letter. The paper, handwriting, seal—all were undoubtedly his. "Plavacek!" he bellowed. "I want you to tell me what happened on your way here."

Plavacek, being a kind and trusting soul, hid nothing; he told of how he had lost his way and how he had passed the night in a cottage in the forest.

"You mentioned an old woman, what was she like?" asked the king.

From Plavacek's description the king knew it was the very same woman who, twenty years before, had foretold the marriage of the princess to the charcoal-burner's son. The king debated a moment, then said, "What is done is done. But you will not become my son-in-law so easily. No, by faith! As a wedding present you must bring me the three golden hairs from the head of Dède-Vsévède."

In this way the king thought to get rid of his son-in-law Plavacek, whose very presence was distasteful to him. The young fellow kissed his new wife on the cheek and set off. "I'm not sure which way to go," he said to himself, "but my godmother the witch will surely help me."

Yet he found his way easily enough. Plavacek walked on and on and on for a long time over mountain, valley and river, until he reached the shores of the Black Sea. There he found a boat and a boatman.

"May God bless you, Sir," Plavacek said politely.

"And you, too, young traveler. Where are you headed?"

"To Dède-Vsévède's castle. I need the three golden hairs from his head."

"Ah, I see. Well, you are very welcome. It's been quite a weary while that I've been waiting for such a one as you. I have been ferrying passengers across the water these twenty years, and not one of them has done anything to help me. If you promise that you will ask Dède-Vsévède when I shall be released from my toil, I will row you across."

Plavacek promised, and the old boatman rowed him to the opposite shore. He continued his journey on foot until he came in sight of a large town, half in ruins, where a funeral procession was passing by. The king of that country followed his father's coffin, and there were tears running down his cheeks.

Plavacek took off his hat and said, "May God comfort you in your distress."

The king wiped his nose on his sleeve and said, "Thank you, my good man." He glanced at Plavacek's well-worn clothes in curiosity and asked, "Where are you going?"

"To the house of Dède-Vsévède. I need the three golden hairs that grow on his head."

"Did you say the house of Dède-Vsévède? Indeed! What a pity you did not get here sooner. We have long been expecting such a messenger as you. Come and see me by and by."

The procession continued down the road to the cemetery, and after the funeral was over Plavacek went to court to present himself to the king.

"I understand that you are on your way to the house of Dède-Vsévède. I have an apple tree here that bears the Fruit of Everlasting Youth. If one of these apples is eaten by a man, even though he lay in his death bed, the fruit will cure him and make him young again. But for the last twenty years neither fruit nor flower has been found on this tree. When you see Dède-Vsévède, will you ask him what the cause of it is?"

"That I will," said Plavacek, "with pleasure."

Plavacek continued his journey, and as he went he came to a large and beautiful city where all was sad and silent. Near the gate was an old man who leaned on a stick and walked with difficulty.

"May God bless you, Old Man," said Plavacek.

"And you, too, my handsome young traveler. Where are you headed?"

"To the palace of Dède-Vsévède, I seek his three golden hairs."

"Ah, you are the messenger I have so long waited for. Will you allow me to take you to my master the king?"

When they arrived at the palace, the king said, "I hear you are an ambassador to Dède-Vsévède. We have here a well, the water of which renews itself. So wonderful are the effects of this water that invalids are immediately cured when they drink it. A few drops sprinkled on a corpse immediately bring the dead man to life again. But for the past twenty years the well has remained dry. If you will ask Dède-Vsévède how the flow of water may be restored, I will reward you royally."

Plavacek promised he would do so, and left with the good wishes of all the court. He continued to travel though deep, dark forests, in the midst of which might be seen a large meadow; out of it grew lovely flowers, and in the center stood a castle built of gold. It was the home of Dède-Vsévède. So brilliantly it shone that it seemed to be built of fire. When he entered the courtyard there was no one there but an old woman spinning.

She looked up and smiled at him. "Good day, Plavacek, I am happy to see you again." It was his godmother, the woman who had given him shelter in her cottage when he was the bearer of the king's letter. "Tell me what brings you such a great distance."

"The king will not have me for a son-in-law until I perform a great deed. He sent me out to gather the three golden hairs from the head of Dède-Vsévède. My journey led me here."

The Fate Sister laughed. "Dède-Vsévède, indeed! Why, I am his mother. It is the Shining Sun himself that you seek. He is a child at dawn, a grown man at noon, and a decrepit old man—looking as if he had lived a hundred years—at sunset. All the same, I will see that you have the three hairs from his head; I am not your godmother for nothing! But you must not remain here. My boy is a good lad, yet when he comes home he is hungry and in a foul mood; he would probably order you to be roasted for his supper! No, I will turn one of the empty buckets upside down, and you shall hide underneath it."

Plavacek begged the Fate to obtain from Dède-Vsévède the answers to the three questions he carried with him. "Certainly I will do so, but you must listen to what he says."

Suddenly a blast of wind howled around the palace, and the Sun entered by a western window. He was an old man, and all that was left of his golden hair were three strands. "I smell human flesh!" he bellowed. "Mother, you have a guest here! Shall he be staying for supper?"

"Star of day," she replied, "whom could I have here that you would not see sooner than I? Your daily journeys have caused the scent of human flesh to cling to you like a bad cooking odor. It is always with you when you come home at night."

The old man said nothing, but glowered fiercely at his mother as he sat down to supper. When he had finished he laid his head on his mother's lap and went to sleep. She stroked his hair and as she stroked she plucked one of the golden hairs and threw it on the ground. It fell with a metallic sound, like the vibration of a guitar string.

"What do you want, Mother?" Dède-Vsévède mumbled sleepily.

"Nothing, nothing, my son; I must have fallen asleep myself. What a strange dream I had!"

"Dream, Mother?"

"Yes, I was in a place where there was a well, and the well was fed from a spring, and the water from that well could cure all diseases. Even the dying were restored to health when they drank the water, and the dead came to life when a few drops were sprinkled on their lips. But I was told that the well had been dry for twenty years. Now what do you think must be done to restore the flow of water again?"

"That is simple, Mother. A frog has lodged itself in the opening of the spring; this keeps the water from flowing. Kill the frog, and the water will return to the well. Now go back to sleep so that I may sleep."

Dède-Vsévède was soon snoring, and the old woman pulled out another golden hair from his head, and threw it on the ground.

"Mother! What are you doing?"

"Nothing, my son, nothing at all; I was dreaming again. In my dream I saw a large town, the name of which I've forgotten. In that town grew an apple tree, the fruit of which had the power to make the old young again. Imagine! A single apple eaten by an old man would restore him to the freshness of his youth. But for twenty years this tree has not borne fruit, not even a single blossom! What can make it fruitful again?"

"That is not difficult to fix. A snake is hidden among the roots, destroying the sap. Kill the snake, transplant the tree, and the fruit will grow just as before."

"Oh, I see. I think I can sleep better now," she said.

Dède-Vsévède was again asleep, and the old woman pulled out a third golden hair.

"Now look here, Mother! Why will you not let me sleep?" roared the old man, really vexed; and he would have got up had his mother not stopped him.

"Hush! Lie down, my darling son. Do not disturb yourself. I am sorry I woke you up, but I have had a very strange dream. It seemed to me that I saw a boatman on the shores of the Black Sea, and he complained that he had been rowing back and forth on the water for twenty years without anyone having come to take his place. How much longer must this poor man continue to row?"

"He is a silly fellow, that one! He has but to place his oars in the hands of the first comer and jump ashore. Whoever receives the oars will replace him as ferryman. But leave me alone now, Mother, and do not wake me again—no matter how strange the dream. I have to rise very early, and must first dry the eyes of a princess. The poor thing spends all night weeping for her husband who has been sent by the king to get three of my golden hairs. Can you imagine such a thing! Who would have the nerve to sneak into my home and pluck the hairs from my head?"

"I can't imagine, Dear," the old woman innocently replied.

The next morning the wind whistled around Dède-Vsévède's palace, and instead of an old man, a beautiful child with golden hair awoke on the old woman's lap. It was the glorious Sun. He kissed her good-bye and flew out the eastern window. The old woman turned and said to Plavacek, "Look, here are the three golden hairs. You heard the answers to your questions. May God direct you and send you a prosperous journey. You will not see me again, Godson, for you will have no further need of my help."

Plavacek hugged the old woman and left. On arriving to the town with the dried-up well, he was questioned by the king. "Did you see Dède-Vsévède? What news do you have?"

"Have the well carefully cleaned out," Plavacek replied. "Kill the frog that obstructs the spring, and the wonderful water will flow as before."

The king did as he was advised, and the water returned. Plavacek was given twelve swan-white horses, and as much gold and silver as each could carry.

On reaching the second town, the king there asked Plavacek what news he had brought. "Excellent news!" Plavacek exclaimed. "One could not wish for better. Dig up your apple tree, kill the snake that lies among the roots, transplant the tree, and it will grow apples like those of former times."

All turned out just as the young man said, for no sooner was the tree replanted than it was covered with delicate white blossoms that gave it the appearance of a sea of roses. The delighted king gave him twelve raven-black horses laden with as much wealth as they could carry. Plavacek then journeyed to the shores of the Black Sea. There the boatman questioned him as to the news he brought from Dède-Vsévède.

"Row myself and my twenty-four horses across, and then I shall tell you." When this was done the ferryman learned that he might gain his freedom by placing the oars in the hands of the first traveler who wished to be ferried across.

Plavacek's royal father-in-law could not have been more surprised when he saw Dède-Vsévède's three golden hairs. As for the young princess, she wept tears of joy to see her dear husband again. "How did you get such splendid horses and so much wealth, dear husband?"

"All this represents the price paid for the weariness of spirit I have felt; it is the ready money for hardships endured and services given. I showed one king how to regain possession of Apples of Youth, and to another I told the secret of reopening the spring of water that gives health and life."

"Apples of Youth! Water of Life!" interrupted the king. "I will certainly go and find these treasures for myself. Ah, what joy! After eating these apples I shall become young again; having drunk the Water of Immortality I shall live forever!"

And he started off in search of these fine treasures; but has he succeeded in his quest? No one can say for sure, because no one has seen him since.

The Story of the Plentiful Tablecloth, the Avenging Wand, the Sash that Becomes a Lake, and the Terrible Helmet

Now it once happened that the king's chief herdsman had three sons. Two of these lads were supposed to be very clever and smart, while the youngest was thought to have not a bit of sense between his ears. The older brothers helped their father keep watch over the flocks while the fool, as they called him, was only good for sleeping.

The fool would spend his whole day and night slumbering peacefully on the stove, only getting off when forced to by others, or when he grew too warm on one side and moved to lie on the other, or when, hungry or thirsty, he wanted food and drink.

His father had no love to spare him, and called him a ne'er-do-well. His brothers often dragged him off the stove and took away his food. He would have gone hungry if his mother had not been a kind soul who took pity on her lazy son, and fed him on the sly. "Why should you suffer, my son?" she would ask, stroking his cheek. "You cannot help it if you've been born a fool. It sometimes happens that the wisest of men are not always happy, while the foolish, when harmless and gentle, lead lives of content."

One day, on their return from the fields, the two older brothers dragged the youngest of them off the stove, took him into the yard, and gave him a sound thrashing. They kicked him out onto the road and said, "Get out of here you good-for-nothing fool! You shall have neither food nor lodging until you earn your keep in some way. Bring us a basket of mushrooms from the woods."

The poor lad was so taken by surprise that he could hardly comprehend what his brothers wanted of him. Not until they hit him in the head with a mushroom basket did he understand. After pondering for a while he made his way toward a small oak forest, where everything seemed to have a strange and marvelous appearance, so strange that he did not recognize the place. As he walked he came to a small dead tree stump, on the top of which he placed his cap, saying, "Every tree here raises its head to the skies and wears a good cap of leaves, but you, my poor friend, are bareheaded; you will die of the cold. You must be among your brothers, as I am among mine—a born fool. Take my cap." He then threw his arms round the dead stump, and wept as he tenderly embraced it.

At that moment an oak which stood near began to walk toward him as though it were alive. The poor fellow was frightened, and about to run away, but the oak spoke to him as if it were human, "Stop, don't run away. Listen to me. This withered tree is my son, and up to this time no one has grieved for his dead youth but me. You have watered him with your tears, and in return for your sympathy you shall have anything you ask of me, on saying these words:

'Oh, Oak Tree so green, with acorns of gold,
your friendship to prove I will try;
In Heaven's good name now to beg I'll make bold,
my needs, then, oh kindly supply.'"

From the branches of the tree fell a shower of golden acorns. The fool filled his basket with them, thanked the oak, and hurried back home.

"Well, Fool, where are the mushrooms?" asked the oldest brother.

"I have some mushrooms off the oak in my basket."

The brothers stared at him in amazement. "Acorns? You're dumber than I thought," said the middle brother. "Acorns aren't mushrooms. You'll have to eat them yourself, for you will get nothing else from home. What have you done with your cap?"

"I put it on a poor stump of a tree that stood by the wayside, for his head was uncovered and I was afraid that he might freeze." He then scrambled onto the top of the stove, and as he lay down some of the golden acorns spilled from his basket. So bright they were, that they shone like sunbeams in the room. In spite of the fool's protests, the brothers gathered the acorns and gave them to their father, who hurried to present them to the king, telling him that the youngest son had gathered them in the woods. The king immediately sent a detachment of his guards to the forest to find this wonderful oak tree, but their efforts were fruitless. Although they hunted in every nook and corner of the forest, they couldn't find a single oak that bore acorns of gold.

At first the king was angry, but then he grew calm and sent for the herdsman. "Tell your foolish son that he must bring me, by this evening, a cask filled to the top with golden acorns. If he does this, neither you nor your family will ever lack bread and salt, and you will rest assured that my royal favor will not fail you in time of need."

The herdsman passed the king's message on to his youngest son.

"The king is fond of a good bargain, I see," the fool laughed scornfully. "He does not ask, he commands—and insists upon a fool fetching him acorns of solid gold in return for promises made of air. No, I won't do it."

Neither prayers nor threats would make him change his mind. His brothers dragged him forcefully off the stove, put his coat on him and a new cap, and dragged him into the road, where they gave him a good beating and said, "Now, you stupid louse, be off and be quick. If you return without the golden acorns you shall have neither supper nor bed."

What could the poor man do? For a great while he wept, then crossing himself he went in the direction of the forest. He soon reached the dead stump where his cap still rested, and stepping up to the mother oak, said to her:

"Oh Oak Tree so green, with acorns of gold,
in my helplessness I to thee cry;
In Heaven's great name now to beg I make bold,
my pressing needs pray satisfy."

The oak moved, and said, "Well, the words aren't exactly right, but they will do." Then she shook her branches, but instead of acorns, a tablecloth fell into the fool's hands. The tree continued, "Keep this cloth always in your possession, and for your own use. When you want a benefit by it, you need only say:

'Oh Tablecloth, who for the poor,
the hungry, and thirsty make cheer,
may he who begs from door to door
feed off you without stint or fear.'"

After uttering these words the oak spoke no more, and the fool, bowing low in thanks, turned toward home. On his way he wondered to himself how he should tell his brothers, and what they would say, but above all he thought how his good mother would rejoice to see the feast-giving tablecloth. When he had walked about half the distance home he met an old beggarman who said to him, "Do you see what a ragged old stick of a man I am? For the love of God give me a little money or some bread."

The fool spread his tablecloth on the grass, and inviting the beggar to sit down, said:

"Oh Tablecloth, who for the poor,
the hungry and thirsty, make cheer,
may he who begs from door to door
feed off you without stint or fear."

Then a whistling sound was heard in the air, and overhead something shone brightly. At the same instant a table, spread as for a royal banquet, appeared before them. Upon it were many different kinds of foods, flasks of mead and glasses of the choicest wine. The plate was of gold and silver.

The fool and the beggarman crossed themselves and began to feast. When they had finished, the whistling was again heard, and everything vanished. The fool folded up his table-cloth and went on his way. But the old man said, "If you will give me your tablecloth you shall have this wand in exchange. When you say certain words to it, it will set upon the person or persons pointed out, and give them such a thrashing that to get rid of it they will give you anything they possess."

The fool glanced down at his bruises and thought of his brothers. He exchanged the cloth for the wand, after which they both went their respective ways.

Suddenly the fool remembered that the oak had ordered him to keep the tablecloth for his own use, and that by parting with it he had lost the power of giving his mother an agreeable surprise. So he said to the wand:

> *"Self-propelling, ever-willing, fighting Wand,*
> *run quick and bring*
> *my feast-providing tablecloth back to my hand,*
> *thy praises I'll then sing."*

The wand went off like an arrow after the old man, quickly overtook him, and throwing itself upon him began to beat him dreadfully, crying out in a loud, clear voice, "For others' goods you seem to have a liking. Stop thief, or sure your back I'll keep on striking."

The poor beggar tried to run away, but it was of no use, for the wand followed him, raining so many blows upon his back and shoulders, and repeating the same words over and over and over again. In spite of his anxiety to keep the table-cloth, the thief was forced to throw it away and flee.

The wand brought back the cloth to the fool, and together they all continued toward home. What a surprise was in store for them all! The fool had not walked very far when a traveler, carrying an empty wallet, accosted him saying, "For the love of God, give me a small coin or a morsel of food, for my bag is empty and I am very hungry. I have a long journey yet ahead of me."

The fool again spread his tablecloth on the grass and repeated the charm. Again a whistling was heard in the air, something shone brightly overhead, and a table, spread as for a royal feast, landed before them. It was laid with a numerous variety of dishes and costly wines. The fool and his guest sat down, crossed themselves, and ate to their heart's delight. When they had finished the whistling filled the area and everything vanished. The fool folded the cloth up carefully, and was about to continue his journey when the traveler said, "Will you exchange your tablecloth for my waistband? When you say certain words it will turn into a deep lake, upon which you may float as you will."

"Is that right?" asked the fool. "Will you tell me what these words might be?"

"The words run like this:

'Oh marvelous, wonderful lake-forming belt,
for my safety, and not for my fun,
bear me in a boat on thy waves far from land,
so that I from my foes need not run.'"

The fool thought his father would find it very convenient to always have water on hand for the king's flocks, and so he gave his tablecloth to the man in exchange for the belt, which he wound round his waist. Taking up the wand, he continued home. It wasn't long before the fool remembered he was to keep the tablecloth for himself, and he said to his wand:

"Self-propelling, ever-willing, fighting Wand,
run quick and bring
my feast-providing tablecloth back to my hand,
thy praises I'll then sing."

The wand at once started in pursuit of the poor traveler, and began to beat him about the back and shoulders crying, "For others' goods you seem to have a liking. Stop thief, or sure your back I'll keep on striking."

The man was terrified out of his wits, and he tried to escape the wands blows, but it was of no use. He was forced to throw the tablecloth away and run as fast as his legs would carry him. The wand brought the tablecloth back to his master, who hid it under his coat and rearranged the waistband. Taking the faithful wand in his hand again, he went toward home.

As he walked he thought about how fun it would be to use the wand on his wicked brothers; he thought of his father's pride when he showed him how to get water for his flocks; and he thought of his mother's joy when she saw the feast-giving tablecloth. These pleasant daydreams were interrupted by a soldier, clothed in rags and hobbling along on crutches. He had once been a famous warrior, but now he was broken and covered with scars.

"Misfortune pursues me," he said to the fool. "I was once a brave soldier, and in my youth I fought valiantly. Now I am crippled for life, and on this lonely road have found no one to give me a morsel of food. Take pity on me and share a little bread."

The fool sat down on the grass and spread out his tablecloth. As before, it brought him food and the old soldier was able to eat to his heart's content. The fool was folding up the tablecloth when the soldier asked, "Will you give me your tablecloth in exchange for this six-horned helmet? It will fire itself off and instantly destroy the object pointed at. You need only turn it round on your head and repeat these magic words:

'Oh magic helmet, never thou
dost want for powder nor shot;
allay my fears and fire now
just where I point. Fail me not!'

You will see that it fires off immediately, and even if your enemy were a mile away he would fall."

The fool was delighted with the idea, and thought how useful such a hat would be in any sudden danger. It would even serve him to defend the king, his country or himself. Without thinking he handed the tablecloth to the soldier, put the helmet on his head, took his wand in his hand, and again set his face toward home.

When he had gone but a short distance, he began to think of what the oak had said about not parting with the table-cloth, and of how his dear mother could not now enjoy the pleasant surprise he had been dreaming about. So he sent the wand to fetch back the cloth.

The wand dashed after the soldier, and having reached him began to beat him on the back, crying out, "For others' goods you seem to have a liking. Stop thief, or sure your back I'll keep on striking."

The soldier was still a powerful man, and in spite of his wound turned right about face, intending to give blow for blow, but the wand was too much for him and he soon found that resistance was useless. Overcome by pain rather than fear, he threw away the tablecloth and took to his heels.

The faithful wand brought the tablecloth back to its master who, glad to have it again, turned toward the final stretch home.

He soon left the forest, crossed the fields, and came in sight of his father's house. At a little distance from it his brothers met him and crossly asked, "Well, stupid, where are the acorns? We have waited all day for you to return."

The fool looked at them and laughed heartily. "You dare to show us such disrespect?" the brothers demanded. "Now you shall get a sound thrashing!"

"No! You are the one who will get a thrashing," the fool laughed. He pointed his wand at his brothers and said:

> "Oh self-propelling, ever-willing, fighting Wand
> strike with thy usual fire
> my ever-scolding, teasing, worrying brother band,
> for they have roused my ire."

The wand needed no second bidding, and darting out of his hand began to thrash the brothers soundly, crying out like a reasoning creature, "Your brother has often your blows felt, alack! Now taste it yourselves; hope you like it, whack, whack!"

The brothers were overpowered, and felt all the while as if boiling water were being poured over their heads. Yelling with pain they began to run at full speed, and soon disappeared with clouds of dust flying round them.

The wand then came back to the fool's hand. He went into the house, climbed on the stove, and told his mother all that had happened. Then he shouted:

"Oh Tablecloth, who for the poor,
the hungry, and thirsty, make cheer,
let us within our cottage door
feed off you without stint or fear."

A whistling was heard in the air, something bright shone overhead, and then a table, laid as for a royal banquet, was placed before them, covered with dainty meats, glasses, and bottles of mead and wine. The whole service was of gold and silver. As the fool and his mother were about to begin the feast, the herdsman entered. He stopped, dumb with amazement, but when invited to join them, began to eat and drink with relish. At the end of the meal the whistling was again heard, and everything completely vanished.

The herdsman set off in haste to the court to tell the king of this new marvel. His majesty sent one of his heroes in search of the fool, whom he found stretched on the stove.

"If you value your life, Fool, you'll listen and obey the king's orders," said the king's man. "He commands that you send him your tablecloth, and then you shall have your share of his royal favor."

The fool turned away from the messenger and rolled over to toast his other side.

"If you don't give the king your cloth immediately, you shall always remain a poor fool, and you will, moreover, be treated as a refractory prisoner—we teach them how to behave.

Do you understand what I am saying?"

"Oh yes, I understand," said the fool, and then he chanted his magic words:

"Oh self-propelling, ever-willing, fighting Wand
Go soundly, thrash that man—
The most deceiving, dangerous wretch in all the land
so hurt him all you can."

The wand sprang from the fool's hand with the speed of lightning and struck the messenger three times in the face. He immediately fled, but the wand was after him, hitting him all the while, and crying out:

"Mere promises are children's play,
so do not throw your breath away,
but think of something true to say,
you rogue, when next you come our way."

Defeated and filled with dismay, the messenger returned to the king and told him about the wand, and how badly he had been beaten. When the king heard that the fool possessed such a wand, he wanted it so much that for a time he forgot all about the tablecloth. He sent a band of soldiers with orders to bring back the wand.

When they entered the cottage the fool, as usual, was lying on the stove.

"Deliver the wand to us instantly," they said. "The king is willing to pay any price you ask, but if you refuse we will take it from you by force."

Instead of replying the fool unwound his belt and said:

"Oh marvelous, wonderful lake-forming Band
for my safety, and not for my fun,
bear me in a boat on thy waves far from land,
so that I from my foes need not run."

There was a shimmering in the air, while at the same moment everything around them disappeared, and a beautiful, long, wide and deep lake was seen, surrounded by green fields. Fish with golden scales and eyes of pearl played in the clean water. In the center, in a small skiff, rowed a man whom the soldiers recognized as the fool.

They waited around for some time, looking for a miracle, before running off to tell the king. Now when the king heard there was such a lake, he sent a whole battalion of soldiers to retrieve the belt and take the fool prisoner.

This time they managed to grab him while he slept on the stove, but as they were about to tie his hands he turned his hat round and said:

"Oh, Magic Helmet, never thou
dost want for powder nor shot,
allay my fears and fire now
just where I point. Fail me not!"

Instantly a hundred bullets whistled through the air, amid clouds of smoke and loud reports. Many of the soldiers fell over dead, others took refuge in the woods, still others returned to the king to give account of what had taken place.

The king flew into such a violent rage, furious that they had as yet failed to take the fool. He wished to possess the feast-giving tablecloth, the magic wand, the lake-forming sash, and above all the helmet with six horns. How dare this peasant keep them from him!

He thought for many days on the best means of attaining his desires, and resolved to try the effect of kindness. He sent for the fool's mother. "Tell your fooli—I mean your youngest—son that my charming daughter and I send greetings, and that we shall consider it an honor if he will come here and show us the marvelous things he possesses. Should he feel inclined to make me a present of them, I will give him half my kingdom and will make him my heir. You may also say that my princess, my daughter, will select him for her husband."

The good woman hastened home to her son, whom she advised to accept the king's invitation and show him the treasures. "You could become a prince!" she exclaimed. The fool wrapped the band round his waist, put the helmet on his head, hid the tablecloth in his breast, took his magic wand in his hand, and started off to go to the court.

The king was not there when he arrived, but he was received by the messenger, who saluted him courteously (he still sported many of the wand's bruises). Music played, and the troops paid him military honors. In fact, he was treated far better than he had expected. On being presented to the king he took off his helmet, bowed low and said, "My king, I have come to lay at your feet my tablecloth, belt, wand and helmet. In return for these gifts I beg that your favor may be shown to the most humble of your subjects."

"Tell me then, Fool, what price you want for these goods."

"Not money, Sire. A fool of my sort cares little about money. Did you not promise my mother that you will give me, in exchange, your daughter and half of your kingdom? That is all I want."

After these words, the king's messenger was filled with envy at the good fortune of the fool. Why should he be able to waltz in here and claim the king's daughter when he himself had been here for years and would never be able to wed her? He made a sign for the guards to enter. The soldiers seized the poor fool, dragged him out into the courtyard, and killed him treacherously to the sound of drums and trumpets. Afterward they covered him with earth.

Now it happened that when the soldiers stabbed the youth, his blood spurted out, and some of the tiny drops fell beneath the princess's window. The maiden wept bitterly at the sight, watering the blood-stained ground with her tears. And lo!

A miracle happened; an apple tree grew out of the blood-sprinkled earth. It grew so rapidly that its branches soon touched the windows of her rooms; by noon it was covered with blossoms, while at dusk ripe red apples hung low. As the princess was admiring them she noticed that one of the apples trembled, and when she reached up to touch it, it fell into the bosom of her dress. This she thought was quite funny, and she held the apple in her hand.

The sun set, night had fallen, and everyone in the palace was asleep except for the guard, the messenger, and the princess. The guard, with sword in hand, patrolled up and down the length of the walls. The princess toyed with her pretty red apple, unable to sleep. The messenger, who had gone to bed, was awakened by a sound that made his blood run cold, for the avenging wand stood before him and began to beat him soundly.

"Ow! Ow!" cried the messenger, but no matter where he tried to escape, the wand was able to follow, crying out:

> *"False messenger, you worthless man,*
> *do not so envious be;*
> *why act unjustly, when you can*
> *both just and honest be?*
> *For others' goods why have you such a liking?*
> *You rogue! You thief! Be sure I'll keep on striking."*

The unhappy man wept and cried for mercy, but the wand continued to strike.

The princess was terrified to hear these cries of distress, and she watered the apple with her tears; strange to tell, the apple grew and changed in shape. It continued to change, twisting first one way, and then the other, until it suddenly turned into a handsome young man—the very same one who had been killed that morning.

"My dear, I salute you," said the fool, bowing low before the princess. "The messenger may have caused my death, but your tears have brought me back to life. Your father promised

to give you to me, but I have not yet asked your consent. Are you willing?"

"Yes, yes I am," she smiled, and took his hand in hers.

Just then there was a knock at the door, and the helmet entered the room and placed itself on the fool's head; the sash followed, and wound itself round his waist; then came the tablecloth, which hid itself in one of his pockets; then finally the avenging wand, which placed itself in his hand.

"What is going on here?" the king burst into the room. "I have been chasing these foolish things for hours. I . . . I . . ." As he caught sight of the fool he stopped dead in his tracks. "Oh, I thought you were dead."

The young fellow, fearing the king's wrath, cried out:

"Oh marvelous, wonderful lake-forming Band,
for my safety and not for my fun,
bear us in a boat on thy waves far from land,
so that we from our foes need not run."

There was a shimmering in the air, and then everything disappeared, while on the lawn before the palace stretched a wide, deep lake, in the crystal water of which swam little fish with eyes of pearl and scales of gold. Far away rowed the princess and the fool in a silver skiff. The king stood on the shores of the lake and signaled to them to return, "It's okay, I won't harm you." When they had landed, they knelt at his feet and proclaimed their mutual love. The king sighed and bestowed his blessing, the lake disappeared, and they again found themselves in the princess's apartments.

The king called a special meeting of his council, and he made the fool his heir, betrothed him to his daughter, and put the messenger in prison. The fool gave the king his magic treasures and told him the words to say in each case. And the wedding feast? All the rich and noble of the land were invited to it, and it exceeded in its magnificence any other festival ever seen or heard of.

Imperishable

Once upon a time, ever so many years ago, there lived an old man and an old woman. Very old indeed were they, for they had lived nearly a hundred years. But they took neither joy nor pleasure in anything, and this because they had no children. They were now about to keep the seventy-fifth anniversary of their wedding day, known as the Diamond Wedding, but no guests were invited to share their feast.

As they sat side by side they went over in memory the years of their long life, and as they did so they felt sure that it was to punish them for their sins that God had denied them the sweet happiness of having children about them, and as they thought their tears fell fast. At that moment someone knocked.

"Who is there?" cried the old woman, and ran to open the door. There stood a little old man leaning on a stick, and white as a dove.

"What do you want?" asked the old woman.

"Charity," answered he.

The good old woman was kind-hearted, and she cut her last loaf in two, giving one half to the beggar, who said, "I see you have been weeping, good wife, and I know the reason of your tears; but cheer up, by God's grace you shall be comforted. Though poor and childless today, tomorrow you shall have family and fortune."

When the old woman heard this she was overjoyed, and fetching her husband they both went to the door to invite the old man in. But he was gone, and though they searched for him in every direction they found nothing but his stick lying on the ground. For it was not a poor old beggar, but an angel of God who had knocked. Our good friends did not know this, so they picked up the stick and hurried off to find the old man, with the purpose of returning it. But it seemed as if the stick, like its master, was endowed with some marvelous power, for whenever the old man or the old woman tried to pick it up it slipped out of their hands and rolled along the ground. Thus they followed it into a forest, and at the foot of a shrub which stood close by a stream it disappeared. They hunted all round the shrub thinking to find the stick there, but instead of the stick they came upon a bird's nest containing twelve eggs, and from the shape of the shells it seemed as if the young ones were ready to come forth.

"Pick up the eggs," said the old man, "they will make us an omelette for our wedding feast."

The old woman grumbled a little, but she took the nest and carried it home in her skirt. Fancy their astonishment when at the end of twelve hours there came out, not unfledged birdlings, but twelve pretty little boys. Then the shells broke into tiny fragments which were changed into as many gold pieces. Thus, as had been foretold, the old man and his wife found both family and fortune.

Now these twelve boys were most extraordinary children. When they came out of the shells they seemed to be at least three months old, such a noise did they make, crying and kicking about. The youngest of all was a very big baby with black eyes, red cheeks, and curly hair, and so lively and active that the old woman could hardly keep him in his cradle at all. In twelve hours' time the children seemed to be a year old, and could walk about and eat anything.

Then the old woman made up her mind that they should be baptized, and thereupon sent her husband to fetch the priest without delay; and the Diamond Wedding was celebrated at the same time as the christening. For a short time their joy was clouded over by the disappearance of the youngest boy, who was his parents' favorite. They had begun to weep and mourn for him as if he were lost, when suddenly he was seen to come from out of the sleeves of the priest's cassock, and was heard to speak these words, "Never fear, dear parents, your beloved son will not perish."

The old woman kissed him fondly and handed him to his godfather, who presented him to the priest. So they had named him Niezguinek, that is, Imperishable. The twelve boys went on growing at the rate of six weeks every hour, and at the end of two years were fine strong young men. Niezguinek, especially, was of extraordinary size and strength. The good old people lived happily and peacefully at home while their sons worked in the fields. On one occasion the latter went plowing; and while the eleven eldest used the ordinary plow and team of oxen, Niezguinek made his own plow, and it had twelve plowshares and twelve handles, and to it were harnessed twelve teams of the strongest working oxen. The others laughed at him, but he did not mind, and turned up as much ground as his eleven brothers put together.

Another time when they went haymaking and his brothers used the ordinary scythes, he carried one with twelve blades, and managed it so cleverly, in spite of the jests of his companions, that he cut as much grass as all of them together. And again, when they went to turn over the hay, Niezguinek used a rake with twelve teeth, and so cleared twelve plots of ground with every stroke. His haycock, too, was as large as a hill in comparison with those of his brothers. Now, the day after the making of the haycocks, the old man and his wife happened to be in the fields, and they noticed that one haycock had disappeared; so thinking wild horses had made off with it, they advised their sons to take turns in watching the place.

The eldest took his turn first, but after having watched all night fell asleep toward morning, when he awoke to find another haycock missing. The second son was no more fortunate in preventing the disappearance of the hay than the eldest, while the others succeeded no better; in fact, of all the twelve haycocks, there only remained the largest, Niezguinek's, and even that had been meddled with.

When it was the youngest's turn to watch, he went to the village blacksmith and got him to make an iron club weighing two hundred and sixty pounds; so heavy was it that the blacksmith and his assistants could hardly turn it on the anvil. In order to test it, Niezguinek whirled it round his head and threw it up in the air, and when it had nearly reached the ground he caught it on his knee, upon which it was smashed to atoms. He then ordered another weighing four hundred and eighty pounds, and this the blacksmith and his men could not even move. Niezguinek had helped them to make it, and when finished he tested it in the same manner as the first. Finding it did not break he kept it, and had in addition a noose plaited with twelve strong ropes. Toward nightfall he went to the field, crouched down behind his haycock, crossed himself, and waited to see what would happen. At midnight there was a tremendous noise which seemed to come from the east, while in that direction appeared a bright light. Then a white mare, with twelve colts as white as herself, trotted up to the haycock and began to eat it. Niezguinek came out of his hiding place, and throwing the noose over the mare's neck, jumped on her back and struck her with his heavy club. The terrified creature gave the signal to the colts to escape, but she herself, hindered by the noose, out of breath, and wounded by the club, could not follow, but sank down on the earth saying, "Do not choke me, Niezguinek."

He marveled to hear her speak, and loosened the noose. When she had taken breath she said, "Knight, if you give me my liberty you shall never repent it. My husband, the Dappled Horse with Golden Mane, will cruelly revenge himself upon you when he knows I am your prisoner; his strength and swiftness are so great you could not escape him. In exchange for my freedom I will give you my twelve colts, who will serve you and your brothers faithfully."

On hearing their mother neigh the colts returned and stood with bent heads before the young man, who released the mare, and led them home. The brothers were delighted to see Niezguinek return with twelve beautiful white horses, and each took the one that pleased his fancy most, while the thinnest and weakest looking was left for the youngest.

The old couple were happy in the thought that their son was brave as well as strong. One day it occurred to the old woman that she would like to see them all married, and to have the house merry with her daughters-in-law and their children. So she called upon her gossips and friends to talk the matter over, and finally persuaded her husband to be of the same opinion. He called his sons around him and addressed them thus: "Listen to me, my sons. In a certain country lives a celebrated witch known as Old Yaga. She is lame, and travels about in an oaken trough. She supports herself on iron crutches, and when she goes abroad carefully removes all traces of her steps with a broom. This old witch has twelve beautiful daughters who have large dowries; do your best to win them for your wives. Do not return without bringing them with you."

Both parents blessed their sons, who, mounting their horses, were soon out of sight. All but Niezguinek, who, left alone, went to the stable and began to shed tears.

"Why do you weep?" asked his horse.

"Don't you think I have good reason? Here I have to go a long long way in search of a wife, and you, my friend, are so thin and weak that were I to depend upon your strength I should never be able to join my brothers."

"Do not despair, Niezguinek," said the horse, "not only will you overtake your brothers, but you will leave them far behind. I am the son of the Dappled Horse with the Golden Mane, and if you will do exactly as I tell you I shall be given the same power as he. You must kill me and bury me under a layer of earth and manure, then sow some wheat over me, and when the grain is ripe it must be gathered and some of it placed near my body."

Niezguinek threw his arms round his horse's neck and kissed him fondly, then led him into a yard and killed him with one blow of his club. The horse staggered a moment and then fell dead. His master covered him with a layer of manure and earth, upon which he sowed wheat, as had been directed. It was immediately watered by a gentle rain, and warmed by the heat of the sun's rays. The corn took root and ripened so quickly that on the twelfth day Niezguinek set to work to cut, thresh, and winnow it. So abundant was it that he was able to give eleven measures to his parents, and keeping one for himself, spread it before his horse's bones. In a very short time the horse moved his head, sniffed the air, and began to devour the wheat. As soon as it was finished he sprang up, and was so full of life that he wanted to jump over the fence in one bound. But Niezguinek held him by the mane, and getting lightly on his back, said, "Halt there, my spirited steed, I do not want others to have the benefit of all the trouble I have had with you. Carry me to Yaga's house."

He was of a truth a most magnificent horse, big and strong, with eyes that flashed like lightning. He leapt up into the air as high as the clouds, and the next moment descended in the middle of a field, saying to his master, "As we have first to see Old Yaga, from whom we are still a great way off, we can stop here for a short time. Take food and rest, I will do the same. Your brothers will be obliged to pass us, for we are a good way in front of them. When they come you can go on together to visit the old witch. Remember, though it is difficult to get into her house, it is much more difficult still to get out. But if you would be perfectly safe, take from under my saddle a brush, a scarf, and a handkerchief. They will be of use in helping you to escape, for when you unroll the scarf, a river will flow between you and your enemy. If you shake the brush it will become a thick forest; and by waving the handkerchief it will be changed into a lake. After you have been received into Yaga's house, and your brothers have stabled their horses and gone to bed, I will tell you how to act."

For twelve days Niezguinek and his horse rested and gained strength, and at the end of the time the eleven brothers

came up. They wondered greatly to see the youngest, and said, "Where on earth did you come from? And whose horse is that?"

"I have come from home. The horse is the same I chose at first. We have been waiting here twelve days; let us go on together now."

Within a short time they came to a house surrounded by a high oaken paling, at the gate of which they knocked. Old Yaga peeped out through a chink in the fence and cried, "Who are you? What do you want?"

"We are twelve brothers come to ask the twelve daughters of Yaga in marriage. If she is willing to be our mother-in-law, let her open the door."

The door was opened and Yaga appeared. She was a frightful-looking creature, old as the hills; and being one of those monsters who feed on human flesh, the unfortunate wretches who once entered her house never came out again. She had a lame leg, and because of this she leaned on a great iron crutch, and when she went out removed all traces of her steps with a broom.

She received the young travelers very graciously, shut the gate of the courtyard behind them, and led them into the house. Niezguinek's brothers dismounted, and taking their horses to the stables, tied them up to rings made of silver; the youngest fastened his to a copper ring. The old witch served her guests with a good supper, and gave them wine and hydromel to drink. Then she made up twelve beds on the right side of the room for the travelers, and on the left side twelve beds for her daughters.

All were soon asleep except Niezguinek. He had been warned beforehand by his horse of the danger that threatened them, and now he got up quietly and re-arranged the positions of the twenty-four beds, so that the brothers lay to the left side of the room, and Yaga's daughters to the right. At midnight, Old Yaga cried out in a hoarse voice, "Guzla, play. Sword, strike."

Then were heard strains of sweet music, to which the old woman beat time from her oaken trough. At the same moment a slender sword descended into the room, and passing over the beds on the right, cut off the heads of the girls one by one, after which it danced about and flashed in the darkness.

When the dawn broke the Guzla ceased playing, the sword disappeared, and silence reigned. Then Niezguinek softly aroused his brothers, and they all went out without making any noise. Each mounted his horse, and when they had broken open the yard gate they made their escape at full speed. Old Yaga, thinking she heard footsteps, got up and ran into the room where her daughters lay dead. At the dreadful sight she gnashed her teeth, barked like a dog, tore out her hair by handfuls, and seating herself in her trough as in a car, set off after the fugitives. She had nearly reached them, and was already stretching out her hand to seize them, when Niezguinek unrolled his magic scarf, and instantly a deep river flowed between her and the horsemen. Not being able to cross it she stopped on the banks, and howling savagely began to drink it up.

"Before you have swallowed all that river you will burst, you wicked old witch," cried Niezguinek. Then he rejoined his brothers.

But Old Yaga drank all the water, crossed the bed of the river in her trough, and soon came near the young people. Niezguinek shook his handkerchief, and a lake immediately spread out between them. So she was again obliged to stop, and shrieking with rage began to drink up the water.

"Before you have drunk that lake dry you will have burst yourself," said Niezguinek, and rode after his brothers.

The old vixen drank up part of the water, and turning the remainder into a thick fog, hastened along in her trough. She was once more close upon the young men when Niezguinek, without a moment's delay, seized his brush, and as he waved it in the air a thick forest rose between them. For a time the witch was at a loss to know what to do. On one side she saw Niezguinek and his brothers rapidly disappearing, while she stood on the other hindered by the branches and torn by the thorns of the thick bushes, unable either to advance or retreat. Foaming with rage, with fire flashing from her eyes, she struck right and left with her crutches, crashing trees on all sides, but before she could clear a way, those she was in pursuit of had got more than a hundred miles ahead.

So she was forced to give up, and grinding her teeth, howling, and tearing out her hair, she threw after the fugitives such flaming glances from her eyes that she set the forest on fire, and taking the road home was soon lost to sight.

The travelers, seeing the flames, guessed what had happened, and thanked God for having preserved them from such great dangers. They continued their journey, and by eventide arrived at the top of a steep hill. There they saw a town besieged by foreign troops, who had already destroyed the outer part, and only awaited daylight to take it by storm.

The twelve brothers kept out of sight behind the enemy, and when they had rested and turned out their horses to graze, all went to sleep except Niezguinek, who kept watch without closing an eye. When everything was perfectly still he got up, and calling his horse, said, "Listen; over in that tent sleeps the king of this besieging army, and he dreams of the victory he hopes for on the morrow. How could we send all the soldiers to sleep and get possession of his person?"

The horse replied, "You will find some dried leaves of the Herb of Sleep in the pocket of the saddle. Mount upon my back and hover round the camp, spreading fragments of the plant. That will cause all the soldiers to fall into a sound sleep, after which you can carry out your plans."

Niezguinek mounted his horse, pronouncing these magic words:

"Marvel of strength and of beauty so white,
Horse of my heart, let us go;
Rise in the air, like a bird take thy flight,
Haste to the camp of the foe."

The horse glanced upward as if he saw someone beckoning to him from the clouds, then rose rapidly as a bird on the

wing and hovered over the camp. Niezguinek took handfuls of the Herb of Sleep from the saddle-pockets and sprinkled it all about, upon which all in the camp, including the sentinels, fell at once into a heavy sleep. Niezguinek alighted, entered the tent, and carried off the sleeping king without any difficulty. He then returned to his brothers, unharnessed his horse and lay down to rest, placing the royal prisoner near him. His majesty slept on as if nothing unusual had taken place.

At daybreak the soldiers of the besieging army awoke, and not being able to find their king, were seized with such a panic of terror that they retreated in great disorder. The ruler of the besieged city would not at first believe that the enemy had really disappeared, and indeed went himself to see if it was true. Of a truth there remained nothing of the enemy's camp but a few deserted tents whitening on the plain. At that moment Niezguinek came up with his brothers, and said, "Sire, the enemy has fled, and we were unable to detain them, but here is their king whom we have made prisoner, and whom I deliver up to you."

The ruler replied, "I see, indeed, that you are a brave man among brave men, and I will reward you. This royal prisoner is worth a large ransom to me, so speak. What would you like me to do for you?"

"I should wish, Sire, that my brothers and I might enter the service of your majesty."

"I am quite willing," answered the king. Then, having placed his prisoner in charge of his guards, he made Niezguinek a general, and placed him at the head of a division of his army; the eleven brothers were given the rank of officers.

When Niezguinek appeared in uniform, and with sabre in hand mounted his splendid charger, he looked so handsome and conducted the maneuvers so well that he surpassed all the other chiefs in the country, thus causing much jealousy, even among his own brothers, for they were vexed that the youngest should outshine them, and so determined to ruin him.

In order to accomplish this they imitated his handwriting, and placed such a note before the king's door while Niezguinek was engaged elsewhere. When the king went out he found the letter, and calling Niezguinek to him, said, "I should very much like to have the phonic Guzla you mention in your letter."

"But, Sire, I have not written anything about a Guzla," said he.

"Read the note then. Is it not in your handwriting?"

Niezguinek read:

"In a certain country, within the house of Old Yaga, is a marvelous Guzla: if the king wishes, I will fetch it for him. Niezguinek"

"It is true," said he, "that this writing resembles mine, but it is a forgery, for I never wrote it."

"Never mind," said the king. "As you were able to take my enemy prisoner you will certainly be able to succeed in getting Old Yaga's Guzla. Go then, and do not return without it, or you will be executed."

Niezguinek bowed and went out. He went straight to the stable, where he found his charger looking very sad and thin, his head drooping before the trough, the hay untouched.

"What is the matter with you, my good steed? What grieves you?"

"I grieve for us both, for I foresee a long and perilous journey."

"You are right, old fellow, but we have to go. And what is more, we have to take away and bring here Old Yaga's Guzla, and how shall we do it, seeing that she knows us?"

"We shall certainly succeed if you do as I tell you." Then the horse gave him certain instructions, and when Niezguinek had mounted he said:

"Marvel of strength and of beauty so white,
Horse of my heart, do not wait on the road;
Rise in the air, like a bird take thy flight,
Haste to the wicked Old Yaga's abode."

The horse arose in the air as if he heard someone calling to him from the clouds, and flitting rapidly along passed over several kingdoms within a few hours, thus reaching Old Yaga's dwelling before midnight. Niezguinek threw the Leaves of Sleep in at the window, and by means of another wonderful herb caused all the doors of the house to open. On entering he found Old Yaga fast asleep, with her trough and iron crutches beside her, while above her head hung the magic sword and Guzla.

While the old witch lay snoring with all her might, Niezguinek took the Guzla and leapt on his horse, crying:

"Marvel of strength and of beauty so white,
Horse of my heart, while I sing,
Rise in the air, like a bird take thy flight,
Haste to the court of my king."

Just as if the horse had seen something in the clouds, he rose swift as an arrow, and flew through the air, above the fogs. The same day about noon he neighed before his own manger in the royal stable, and Niezguinek went in to the king and presented him with the Guzla. On pronouncing the two words, "Guzla, play," strains of music so gay and inspiring were heard that all the courtiers began dancing with one another. The sick who listened were cured of their diseases, those who were in trouble and grief forgot their sorrows, and all living creatures were thrilled with a gladness such as they had never felt before. The king was beside himself with joy; he loaded Niezguinek with honors and presents, and, in order to have him always at court, raised him to a higher rank in the army. In this new post he had many men under him, and he showed much exactitude in drill and other matters, punishing somewhat severely when necessary. He made, too, no difference in the treatment of his brothers, which angered them greatly, and caused them to be still more jealous and to plot against him. So they again imitated his handwriting and composed another letter, which they left at the king's door. When his majesty had read it he called Niezguinek to him and said, "I should much like to have the marvelous sword you speak of in your letter."

"Sire, I have not written anything about a sword," said Niezguinek.

"Well, read it for yourself." And he read:

"In a certain country within the house of Old Yaga is a sword that strikes of its own accord: if the king would like to have it, I will engage to bring it to him. Niezguinek"

"Certainly," said Niezguinek, "this writing resembles mine, but I never wrote those words."

"Never mind, as you succeeded in bringing me the Guzla you will find no difficulty in obtaining the sword. Leave right away, and do not return without it at your peril."

Niezguinek bowed and went to the stable, where he found his horse looking very thin and miserable, with his head drooping.

"What is the matter, my horse? Do you want anything?"

"I am unhappy because I foresee a long and dangerous journey."

"You are right, for we are ordered to return to Yaga's house for the sword. But how can we get hold of it? Doubtless she guards it as the apple of her eye."

The horse answered, "Do as I tell you and all will be right." And he gave him certain instructions. Niezguinek came out of the stable, saddled his friend, and mounting him said:

"Marvel of strength and of beauty so white,
Horse of my heart, do not wait on the road;
Rise in the air, like a bird take thy flight,
Haste to the wicked old witch's abode."

The horse rose immediately as if he had been beckoned to by someone in the clouds, and passing swiftly through the air, crossed rivers and mountains, till at midnight he stopped before Old Yaga's house.

Since the disappearance of the Guzla, the sword had been placed on guard before the house, and whoever came near it was cut to pieces.

Niezguinek traced a circle with holy chalk, and placing himself on horseback in the center of it, said:

"Sword who of thyself can smite,
I come to brave thy ire;
Peace or war upon this site
Of thee I do require.
If thou canst conquer, thine my life;
Should I beat thee, then ends this strife."

The sword clinked, leapt into the air, and fell to the ground divided into a thousand other swords, which ranged themselves in battle array and began to attack Niezguinek. But it was in vain, they were powerless to touch him, for on reaching the chalk-traced circle they broke like wisps of straw. Then the sword-in-chief, seeing how useless it was to go on trying to wound him, submitted itself to Niezguinek and promised him obedience. Taking the magic weapon in his hand, he mounted his horse and said:

"Marvel of strength and of beauty so white,
Horse of my heart, while I sing,
Rise in the air, like a bird take thy flight,
Back to the court of my king."

The horse started with renewed courage, and by noon was eating his hay in the royal stables. Niezguinek went home to the king and presented him with the sword. While he was rejoicing over it one of his servants rushed in quite out of breath and said, "Sire, your enemies who attacked us last year, and whose king is your prisoner, surround our town. Being unable to redeem their sovereign, they have come with an immense army, and threaten to destroy us if their king is not released without ransom."

The king armed himself with the magic sword, and going outside the city walls, said to it, as he pointed to the enemy's camp, "Magic Sword, smite the foe."

Immediately the sword clinked, leapt flashing in the air, and fell in a thousand blades that threw themselves on the camp. One regiment was destroyed during the first attack, another was defeated in the same way, while the rest of the terrified soldiers fled and completely disappeared. Then the king said, "Sword, return to me."

The thousand swords again became one, and so returned to its master's hand.

The victorious king came home filled with joy. He called Niezguinek to him, loaded him with gifts, and assuring him of his favor, made him the highest general of his forces. In carrying out the duties of this new post Niezguinek was often obliged to punish his brothers, who became more and more enraged against him, and took counsel together how they might bring about his downfall.

One day the king found a letter by his door, and after reading it he called Niezguinek to him and said, "I should very much like to see Princess Sudolisu, whom you wish to bring me."

"Sire, I do not know the lady, and have never spoken to her."

"Here, look at your letter." Niezguinek read:

"Beyond the nine kingdoms, far beyond the ocean, within a silver vessel with golden masts lives Princess Sudolisu: if the king wishes it, I will seek her for him. Niezguinek

"It is true the writing is like unto mine; nevertheless, I neither composed the letter nor wrote it."

"No matter," answered the king. "You will be able to get this princess, as you did the Guzla and the sword: if not, I will have you killed."

Niezguinek bowed and went out. He entered the stable where stood his horse looking very weak and sad, with his head bent down.

"What is the matter, dear horse? Are you in want of anything?"

"I am sorrowful," answered the horse, "because I foresee a long and difficult journey."

"You are right, for we have to go beyond the nine kingdoms, and far beyond the ocean, to find Princess Sudolisu. Can you tell me what to do?"

"I will do my best, and if it is God's will we shall succeed. Bring your club of four hundred and eighty pounds weight, and let us be off."

Niezguinek saddled his horse, took his club, and mounting said:

"Marvel of strength and of beauty so white,
Horse of my heart, do not lag on the road;
Rise in the air, through the clouds take thy flight,
Haste to Princess Sudolisu's abode."

Then the horse looked up as if there were something he wanted in the clouds, and with a spring flew through the air, swift as an arrow; and so by the second day they had passed over ten kingdoms, and finding themselves beyond the ocean, halted on the shore. Here the horse said to Niezguinek, "Do you see that silver ship with golden masts that rides on the waves yonder? That beautiful vessel is the home of Princess Sudolisu, thirteenth daughter of Old Yaga. For after the witch had lost the Guzla and magic sword she feared to lose her daughter too: so she shut her up in that vessel, and having thrown the key thereof into the ocean, sat herself in her oaken trough, where with the help of the iron crutches she rows round and round the silver ship, warding off tempests, and keeping at a distance all other ships that would approach it.

"The first thing to be done is to get the diamond key that opens the ship. In order to procure this you must kill me, and then throw into the water one end of my entrails, by which bait you will trap the King of the Lobsters. Do not set him free until he has promised to get you the key, for it is this key that draws the vessel to you of its own accord."

"Ah, my beloved steed," cried Niezguinek, "how can I kill you when I love you as my own brother, and when my fate depends upon you entirely?"

"Do as I tell you; you can bring me to life again, as you did before."

Niezguinek caressed his horse, kissed him, and wept over him; then, raising his mighty club, struck him full on the forehead. The poor creature staggered and fell down dead. Niezguinek cut him open, and putting an end of his entrails in the water, he kept hold of it and hid himself in the water-rushes. Soon there came a crowd of crawfish, and amongst them a gigantic lobster as large as a year-old calf. Niezguinek seized him and threw him on the beach. The lobster said, "I am king of all the crawfish tribe. Let me go, and I will give you great riches for my ransom."

"I do not want your riches," answered Niezguinek, "but in exchange for your freedom give me the diamond key which belongs to the silver ship with the golden masts, for in that vessel dwells Princess Sudolisu."

The King of the Crawfish whistled, upon which myriads of his subjects appeared. He spoke to them in their own language, and dismissed one, who soon returned with the magic diamond key in his claws.

Niezguinek loosed the King of the Crawfish, and hiding himself inside his horse's body as he had been instructed, lay in wait. At that moment an old raven, followed by his nestlings, happened to pass near, and attracted by the horse's carcass, he called to his young ones to come and feast with him. Niezguinek seized the smallest bird and held it firmly.

"Let my birdling go," said the old raven. "I will give you in return anything you like to ask."

"Fetch me then three kinds of water, the Life-giving, the Curing, and the Strengthening."

The old raven started off, and while awaiting his return Niezguinek, who still held the ravenling, questioned him as to where he had come from and what he had seen on his travels, and in this way heard news of his brothers.

When the father bird returned, carrying with him the bottles filled with the marvelous waters, he wanted to have his nestling back.

"One moment more," said Niezguinek, "I want to be sure that they are of the right sort."

Then he replaced the entrails in the body of his horse and sprinkled him first with the Life-giving, then with the Curing, and finally with the Strengthening Water, after which his beloved steed leapt to his feet full of strength and cried, "Ah! How very soundly I have slept."

Niezguinek released the young raven and said to his horse, "For sure, you would have slept to all eternity, and have never seen the sun again, if I had not revived you as you taught me."

While speaking he saw the marvelous ship sparkling white in the sun. She was made entirely of pure silver, with golden masts. The rigging was of silk, the sails of velvet, and the whole was enclosed in a casing of impenetrable steel network. Niezguinek sprang down to the water's edge armed with his club, and rubbing his forehead with the diamond key, said:

"Riding on the ocean waves a magic ship I see;
Stop and change thy course, oh ship,
here I hold the key.

Obey the signal known to thee,
and come at once direct to me."

The vessel turned right around and came at full speed toward land, and right onto the bank, where it remained motionless.

Niezguinek smashed in the steel network with his club, and opening the doors with the diamond key, there found Princess Sudolisu. He made her unconscious with the Herb of Sleep, and lifting her before him on his horse, said:

"Marvel of strength and of beauty so white,
Horse of my heart, while I sing;
Swift as an arrow through space take thy flight,
Straight to the court of my king."

Then the horse, as if he saw some strange thing in the clouds, lifted himself in the air and began to fly through space so rapidly that in about two hours he had crossed rivers, mountains, and forests, and had reached his journey's end.

Although Niezguinek had fallen violently in love with the princess himself, he took her straight to the royal palace and introduced her to the king.

Now she was so exquisitely beautiful that the monarch was quite dazzled by looking at her, and being thus carried away by his admiration, he put his arm around her as if to caress her, but she rebuked him severely.

"What have I done to offend you, Princess? Why do you treat me so harshly?"

"Because in spite of your rank you are ill-bred. You neither ask my name nor that of my parents, and you think to take possession of me as if I were but a dog or a falcon. You must understand that he who would be my husband must have triple youth: that of heart, soul, and body."

"Charming Princess, if I could become young again we would be married directly."

She replied, "But I have the means of making you so, and by help of this sword in my hand. For with it I will pierce you to the heart, then cut up your body into small pieces, wash them carefully, and join them together again. And if I breathe upon them you will return to life young and handsome, just as if you were only twenty years of age."

"Oh, indeed! I should like to know who would submit to that; first make trial of Sir Niezguinek here."

The princess looked at him, whereupon he bowed and said, "Lovely Princess, I willingly submit, although I am young enough without it. In any case life without you would be valueless."

Then the princess took a step toward him and killed him with her sword. She cut him up in pieces and washed these in pure water, after which she joined them together again and breathed upon them. Instantly Niezguinek sprang up full of life and health, and looked so handsome and bright that the old king, who was dreadfully jealous, exclaimed, "Make me, too, young again, Princess; do not lose a moment."

The princess pierced him to the heart with her sword, cut him up into little pieces, and, opening the window, threw them out, at the same time calling the king's dogs, who quickly ate them up. Then she turned to Niezguinek and said, "Proclaim yourself king, and I will be your queen."

He followed her advice, and within a short time they were married; his brothers, whom he had pardoned, and his parents having been invited to the wedding joined them. On their way back from the church, the magic sword suddenly clinked, and, flashing in the air, divided itself into a thousand swords that placed themselves on guard as sentinels all round the palace. The Guzla, too, began to play so sweetly and gaily that every living thing began to dance for joy.

The festival was magnificent. I myself was there, and drank freely of wine and mead, and although not a drop went into my mouth, my chin was quite wet.